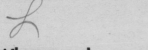

What people are saying about
THE ROSE TATTOO:

Dear Reader,

When I was little, my sister and I played the board game Mystery Date. The point of the game is to win a date with this perfect guy in a tux. My sister didn't like playing with me because I always wanted her to win—not a very common occurrence between siblings. Losing meant I could open the door to glimpse my true love—the Surfer Dude. I didn't care that the rules said he was a loser. At the age of eleven, I dreamed that I would one day be Mrs. Surfer Dude.

In *The Wrong Man*, lawyer Haley Jenkins is as determined to wait until she finds her dream man. She has only one rule—no cops. Detective Dalton Ross wouldn't mind settling down. He has only one rule— no lawyers. I couldn't make it too easy for them though. Thanks to one of my favorite characters, waitress Susan Taylor, Haley and Dalton find love only after they find a missing woman. The mystery isn't so much the who, but the why and the when. I did this because I wanted these characters to have to rack their brains to figure out this puzzle. By uniting Haley's methodical mind with Dalton's savvy street sense, they achieve their goal.

I had a lot of fun showing these two people that it can be more fun when you forget the rules and listen to your heart. A lesson I learned from my first true love—Surfer Dude.

I hope you enjoy this newest tale from THE ROSE TATTOO.

I'd love to hear from you. You can write to me at P.O. Box 1624, Pasadena, MD 21122-6434.

Fondly,

Kelsey Roberts

Kelsey Roberts

The Wrong Man

Harlequin Books

TORONTO • NEW YORK • LONDON
AMSTERDAM • PARIS • SYDNEY • HAMBURG
STOCKHOLM • ATHENS • TOKYO • MILAN
MADRID • WARSAW • BUDAPEST • AUCKLAND

For Kyle—I hope you enjoy middle school.
And for Bob—I hope you enjoy your
53rd consecutive first day of school.

ISBN 0-373-22429-X

THE WRONG MAN

Copyright © 1997 by Rhonda Harding-Pollero

Drawing by Linda Harding Shaw

CAST OF CHARACTERS

Haley Jenkins—Barbie with a law degree and an attitude.

Detective Dalton Ross—The hero with a badge—and an attitude of his own.

Barbara Prather—Skipper to Haley's Barbie; an ad exec—with an attitude, of course.

Susan Taylor—Haley's friend who is a few crystals short of a necklace.

Rose Porter—The proprietor of the Rose Tattoo...who defies description.

Shelby Tanner—The perfect, biscuit-baking Southern woman.

Claire Benedict—Haley's missing friend, who would do anything to have a baby.

Justin Benedict—Claire's ex-husband, ex-con and general slimeball.

Greg Walsh—Claire's ex-boyfriend and general slimeball (see a pattern here?).

Michael Dixon, M.D.—Claire's fertility specialist.

Lawrence Betterman, III—Haley's boss.

Jonathan Phelps—Haley's other boss, who has a few secrets.

Sergeant Lauer—A not-so-good cop.

Chapter One

Haley Jenkins hopped out onto the porch, letting the thick wooden door slam behind her as she fought a valiant battle to pull the strap of her sandal over her heel. Her curse was muffled by the shoulder strap of her purse, which dangled precariously between her teeth.

The energy-zapping humidity that settled over her like a blanket didn't help her mood, nor did the fact that she still hadn't managed to get her shoe on properly. Heat floated from every surface, making her feel as if she was looking out at the world through a lens beneath dull, gray water.

"Thank you, Claire," she grumbled as she pulled her cluttered key chain from the depths of her handbag as she reached her car.

The car's interior was even more stifling and she could feel beads of perspiration begin to trickle between her shoulder blades.

Glancing in the rearview mirror she determined

two things—it was safe to pull away from the curb
and she was having a very bad hair day. "I'm moving north!"

Her car sputtered once before darting forward,
leaving a trail of bluish smoke she was pretty sure
was a bad car omen. The air conditioner spewed hot,
musty-smelling air for the first few miles before finally offering some much needed relief from
Charleston weather in mid-August. She maneuvered
her way through the early evening traffic, heading
for the Rose Tattoo. The heat followed her.

Haley secretly resented being summoned out on a
night like this. *I should have called Claire and Susan
and begged off,* she thought to herself, but the wuss
in her had triumphed, preventing her from doing it.

"Thank you, Mother," she grumbled, knowing
full well that her talent for loading herself with guilt
was directly traceable to her early childhood training
to be kind to others.

Not only had Claire directed Haley to appear at
the Rose Tattoo at seven-fifteen sharp, her message
also included a directive that she go completely out
of her way to collect Barbara.

Despite all this, Haley's mood began to improve
now that the air-conditioning was working. By the
time she turned on to the tree-lined cul-de-sac where
Barbara lived, her smile was more felt than forced.

Pulling into a spot in front of Barbara's condo, she
honked the horn. The front door opened even before

the sound had echoed and died. Barbara, dressed in her usual brightly colored, perfectly tailored suit, emerged from number 401. She was having a good hair day. Her long red hair was neatly braided and fastened into a bun at the nape of her neck. She looked every inch the efficient upwardly mobile advertising rep.

"We must be entering the first stages of Armageddon," Barbara said, dabbing at the small droplets of perspiration above her lip. "Did Claire say what this dinner is all about?"

"I didn't talk to her—she left a message."

"How'd she sound?" Barbara's tone lingered somewhere between cautious and callous. "I know today was *the day*."

"Happy. No, excited, I think." Haley steered her car back in the direction of the ozone-hidden haze of town.

"You know that can only mean one thing," Barbara said.

Haley watched as her friend's features folded into an expression of acute disgust.

"Cut her a break. She's looking for something to make her feel useful and loved."

"Then she should get a dog. You'd think she would have better things to concentrate on—like *all* that money." The laughter they shared was tainted slightly, by deep-seated envy.

Claire's inherited fortune had always been the barometer Barbara and Haley used to rank their successes. Of course, Claire had tons of money, but her wealth was tempered by a long history of disastrous personal relationships.

They arrived at the Rose Tattoo. It was one of the most beautifully restored Charleston Single Homes, even if the proprietor was a little left of center. Haley grinned when she thought of Rose Porter. She couldn't imagine anyone but that cantankerous woman employing her longtime friend Susan.

Susan came rushing forward as soon as they had managed to push through the line of unhappy people waiting for tables.

"You're on time!" Susan exclaimed. "I've got ten more minutes on my shift, but there's a table reserved for us out on the porch."

"The porch?" Barbara moaned. "It's got to be a hundred degrees out there."

Susan's mouth puffed into a pout. "Rose wouldn't let me reserve one of the inside tables and Claire was really insistent when she called this meeting."

"Then where is she?" Haley asked.

"She'll be here," Susan promised with her usual forgiveness of the flaws of others.

Haley suspected that Susan's easy acceptance of other people's shortcomings was due to her awareness of her own eclectic leanings. Susan's latest fixation had something to do with spiritual housecleanings and white witches. Hopefully that would be an improvement over pyramids, channeling, crystals and auras.

After five minutes of enjoying the air-conditioning, and with Claire nowhere to be found, Barbara and Haley went to their table and settled in with a bottle of moderately priced wine.

The time passed slowly and Haley's stomach growled louder with each second.

"I'm giving Claire another ten minutes, then I order," Barbara announced.

"She might be stuck in traffic," Susan suggested as she joined them, poured herself some wine and swirled the contents of her glass.

"Knowing Claire, she's probably stopping people on the street to give them the latest update on her quest for personal reproduction."

"Barbara!" Haley tried to sound affronted through teeth clenched tight in an attempt to stifle the giggle she felt bubbling in her throat.

"Oh, c'mon, Haley." Barbara waved her hand in a highly polished gesture that was probably an effective tool in those sales meetings she often discussed. "I love Claire, but I'm sick to death of hearing the Ovary Oratory." Barbara clasped one hand over her heart and the other rested melodramatically flat against her forehead.

A chuckle slipped past the defensive line of Haley's lips. "Okay, I'll grant you that she's been a little obsessive about the topic lately."

"Obsessive!" Barbara parroted. She leaned forward, resting her elbows against the linen tablecloth. "I'm all for Claire having a baby. God knows it can't be any worse than when she dropped out of school to marry Justin the Thief. I'm just sick of discussing it every time I see the woman. You watch." Barbara's pretty green eyes narrowed with accusation. "Twenty bucks says Claire will bring up the subject of reproduction within five minutes of her arrival."

Haley smiled as she thought of Claire; the old familiar feelings of inferiority washed over her. Claire Benedict, her childhood companion, her trusted confidante, had this uncanny ability to make her feel like a troll. *And she's probably having an excellent hair day,* Haley thought miserably. Claire always looked perfect and feminine, two areas that had always seemed to elude Haley, no matter how hard she tried.

Mark, the waiter who had spent the better part of a half hour topping off their wineglasses, scurried over and presented Susan with one of the hand-printed menus before pouring some zinfandel into her glass.

"We'd better order," Haley said.

Mark shot her a grateful look over his shoulder.

In her peripheral vision she watched Barbara's normally complacent features strain. "I've had a long day. Whatever it is she wanted, she can tell me over dessert. I'm not waiting another second."

When Susan's features froze with obvious hurt at

Barbara's sarcastic tone, Haley looked heavenward and prayed for peace. Her hopes for a nice, quiet dinner were slowly being replaced by a real and fervent hope that her two good friends wouldn't be reduced to a shouting match in the middle of the restaurant.

"Please, Barbara?" Susan pleaded. "Don't start. Rose will have a fit if you cause a scene when Claire shows up. And you know she'll get here, she just gets sidetracked sometimes. Besides, I'm sensing an awful lot of red in your aura, Barbara. You really should try to get that under control."

"I'll work on it," Barbara said without even a hint of sincerity.

"Is there something wrong with consulting specialists?" Susan asked Barbara, using the inflection in her tone like a gauntlet.

"Of course there's nothing wrong with it," Haley insisted. She was uncomfortable. Then again, playing peacekeeper always made her feel like June Cleaver. "I'm sure Barbara doesn't think so either."

"There's nothing wrong with consulting specialists, per se," Barbara agreed. "I just think deciding to become a single parent with her track record is absurd. Justin was a criminal, and she's told me nothing but horrifying stories about her latest guy." Barbara turned to Haley and asked, "Have you talked to her about him? He sounds dangerous from what little I know."

Haley nodded. "She's finally agreed to get a restraining order. We're supposed to get together later this week and I'm going to help her with the paperwork."

"Good," Susan breathed. "I saw what Destiny went through when she had that crazy man after her."

Haley forced a lightness to her tone. "Claire has been pretty tight-lipped about it, but I think he's finally done something that's pushed her over the edge."

"Do you know his name yet?" Barbara asked, then turning to Susan with a playful grin she added, "Wait, we don't need to ask his name, can't you tune him in on one of your channels? Like the Psycho Channel? Or the Stalker Channel?"

"Don't make fun of me," Susan answered. "It's not channels, it is *channeling*."

"Forgive me," Barbara said. "My mistake."

The air had grown somewhat thick just as Mark returned, pad and pen poised. "Are you ladies ready to order?"

"If you two are going to bicker, I'm going to ask to be moved to a table for one."

Haley's companions looked contrite and nodded, which she supposed meant everyone was going to stay and play nicely in the sandbox.

"I'm sorry, Susan," Barbara said. "I guess it just bothers me to think you might be stepping onto yet

another treadmill. You do seem to belong to the psy-
chic-fixation-of-the-month club.'' Barbara reached
out and patted Susan's hand. The gesture was just
enough to allow Haley to relax the knotted muscles
of her empty stomach.

Mark stood with an air of impatience, glowering
at Susan. After he deposited a basket of rolls in the
center of the table, they took turns ordering. Throwing regard for her cholesterol level out the window,
Haley happily settled on a petit filet and ordered extra béarnaise, justifying her actions by telling herself
that steak wasn't something she would normally prepare at home. Then again, she considered anything
that required more than three minutes on high in the
microwave a major culinary undertaking.

''I wonder where she is?'' Haley said as she
glanced around the crowded restaurant. ''Surely her
appointment with that doctor couldn't take this
long.''

''Maybe she's getting to know him personally,''
Barbara joked. ''If he's cute and the timing is right,
the two of them *could* just do it the old-fashioned
way.''

''That's gross,'' Susan wailed. ''He's a doctor and
she's his patient. They can't do it. That would be
unethical and I know Claire is taking this very seriously. She's really checked this guy out and she's
committed to the motherhood thing.''

"Am I the only one here who doesn't hear the tick of her biological clock?"

Haley smiled but didn't answer. To be truthful, she wasn't sure what her feelings were on the subject. Until Claire had announced that she was going to have a baby by artificial insemination, Haley had pretty much left that part of her on the back burner. Now, though, she was suddenly more aware of the fact that she was entering the danger zone. That time when "forty" looms on the horizon and expressions like "if you're going to do it, you'd better get going" popped in and out of her head at the oddest moments.

"It's probably a smart idea," Barbara admitted. "I hear artificial insemination is a big industry these days."

"How's business?" Haley asked Barbara, changing the subject.

"Pretty good. I just signed a contract with Citizens for Peace," she answered.

"Claire gives them a lot of money," Susan said. "She hopes they're successful in getting at least some of those dreadful handguns off the street."

"I'm going to put together a half dozen thirty-second spots."

"That's really great," Haley said, reaching to uncover the basket of rolls. Taking one for herself, she passed them to Susan. "A real winner came across my desk this week." Leaning closer to the center of the table, she continued, ''A client of mine is suing the City for making him ride a horse.''

''Why is he suing the city?'' Barbara asked.

''He's a natural resources officer. The guy asked for a transfer to the mounted division, and now he claims his fear of horses has caused a back injury that prevents him from working.''

''Did he fall off the horse during training?'' Susan asked.

Haley shook her head and felt a mischievous light narrow her eyes. A smile tugged at the corners of her mouth. ''My complainant says he's so afraid of horses that he developed irritable bowel syndrome. That condition then caused him to tense his muscles, which in turn caused the back injury, which in turn has caused him great anguish of mind, and, well...you get the picture.''

''Wait a minute!'' Barbara fought to keep her laughter in check. ''This guy is suing the city because sitting on a horse gives him the runs?''

''Exactly.''

They laughed loud and long enough to earn baleful stares from the adjoining tables. By the time Mark arrived with the food, Haley was busy wiping the remnants of mascara-stained tears from her cheeks. ''I'm going to call Claire,'' she said just as her food was placed in front of her. ''It won't take but a minute.''

It took less than a minute. "No answer at her house, not even the machine."

"That's weird," Susan said.

"I tried her cell phone too, but she must have it turned off." Although she spoke lightly, Haley found she really didn't like the fact that Claire was this late and hadn't called.

"I don't envy you all your careers," Susan said as she poked a chunk of chicken with her fork. "I'm glad I didn't pursue graduate school. I like what I'm doing."

"Like you could do anything else with a degree in philosophy," Barbara observed dryly.

Considering the general mood of her dining companions, Haley was glad when they paid the check and left, although she was guiltily questioning her qualifications as a friend. They'd lingered over dessert, and never once tried to reach Claire again.

By the time she got back home, the outside air temperature had dropped into the more bearable eighties. Without flipping on any lights, she made her way through the maze of construction to the stairway leading to the second floor. She wondered if the original builder of the house had encountered as many construction problems the first time around as she had during the course of the renovations. This was the sixth month of restoration purgatory and the odds were fifty-fifty on what would run out first—her patience or her money.

"Money," she acknowledged as she started up the stairs. By the seventh step, she was peeling clothes off her damp body. In the back of her mind she could hear her high school science teacher's long-ago lecture on the inescapable rise of hot air. *Her name was Mrs. Bagley,* she recalled as she tossed her slip onto the chair next to the bed. Rolling on top of the covers, she reached for the remote.

"The miracle of cable," she said with a sigh, flipping through the fifty-odd channels at her disposal before settling on an old black and white film playing on one of the higher numbers. Setting the automatic timer to turn the set off in an hour, she began to relax, until she noticed the flashing red light on her answering machine.

Pressing the play button, she strained to hear the soft, almost inaudible sound of Claire's voice.

She hit rewind and adjusted the volume. "Haley, you've got to help me. I'm—"

Her panic began where the message abruptly ended. Grabbing the phone, she dialed the emergency operator. She explained the situation and was politely but firmly told that her concerns would be assigned to a detective, who would get in touch with her.

"I don't think you understand," Haley argued. "Ms. Benedict missed dinner and this message sounds as if something terrible might have happened to her."

"I don't think *you* understand," the bored voice

answered. "We don't send out patrol cars to investigate answering machine messages. Do you want me to pass this along to Missing Persons or not?"

"I want you to send someone over to her house to check on her," Haley countered.

"It doesn't work that way, ma'am."

"Fine, I'll do it myself then. I can't begin to tell you how much I appreciate your help. I'm an attorney, so if I find anything out of the ordinary, I'll be sure to mention your name personally when I file suit against the city attorney."

There was a brief pause before the operator relented and asked, "What's the address?"

Haley gave the information as she pulled on a pair of jeans and stuffed her nightshirt into the waistband. She left the portable phone on the table and flew downstairs, grabbed her keys and ran out the door, chased by a whole litany of fears.

Claire owned a huge estate on the outskirts of town and Haley ignored most of the posted speed limit signs getting there. To her surprise, she found a dark blue sedan parked in front of the locked gate.

A man stepped from the car and stood bathed in the floodlights that guarded the ornate iron gates.

He looked in his late thirties, maybe, with thick, unruly dark hair that seemed too long to meet the regulations that went with the unmarked police car. Because of her recent hair-analysis phase, Haley noticed that before she caught the serious expression in his dark hazel eyes.

"Miss Jennings?" he asked.

As he said her name, Haley felt a kind of reaction she had never had before. Taking in his broad shoulders, casually arrogant posture and the angled—no, chiseled—perfection of his features, she found her palms moist. She didn't offer her hand; she walked over and stood next to the keypad on the security panel. "I'm Haley Jenkins. Thanks for meeting me here. I'm really concerned about Claire since getting that message."

In her peripheral vision, she watched as he shrugged off his jacket and tossed it into the car. She noted the dark, horseshoe-shaped perspiration stains beneath the sleeves of his shirt. *Good, this gorgeous man isn't a dream. Fantasy men don't sweat,* she told herself. He isn't completely perfect.

"I'm Detective Ross." Flipping his wallet out of the breast pocket of his shirt, he showed her an official-looking gold shield.

"Detective," she said politely as she entered the code that opened the gates.

"What can I do for you?"

"Just come with me," she answered, not really sure what she wanted him to do now that she was there. "Maybe she's fallen or something and needs help."

"Are you a close friend of Ms. Benedict?" he

asked as he directed a flashlight beam against the driveway in front of them.

"Close enough to know the alarm codes and have my own set of keys," she answered, immediately sorry that had come out sounding so flippant. "I didn't mean to be rude," she added as she sensed him following her up the horseshoe-shaped pavement. "I had a hard time convincing the dispatcher that this was important."

The detective shifted his weight as he stood next to her while she fumbled with the keys, then disabled the alarm.

"Claire?" she called out into the total blackness of the house.

It was then that she felt the warmth of his hand as he gripped her upper arm in order to move ahead of her. It made perfect sense that he should lead the way. He was bigger, had the flashlight, and when she heard him unsnap the holster of his gun, she actually shivered.

"You might want to wait here," he said in a tone that was soft, but definitely a command.

"I'd rather come with you," Haley said.

He turned once, meeting her eyes. She read caution and something that bordered on sympathy as he said, "That probably isn't a good idea."

"Why?" she asked as she half shoved him to peer inside.

There on the foyer, just inside the circle from his light, she saw it. Blood.

Chapter Two

"What do you mean you found blood?"

Dalton remained calm as he studied the woman's expression. It was a mixture of shock, disbelief and definite concern. Barbara Prather wasn't as emotional as Haley, or as attractive.

Rubbing his hands over his face, he silently cursed two things. First, he really hated this part of the job, especially when there was nothing really concrete. Secondly, it annoyed the hell out of him that he was already comparing other women to the standard set by Ms. Haley Jenkins. She was a lawyer. He hated lawyers.

"It wasn't a pool of blood, it was a couple of small drops. I've lost more blood from a paper cut."

Barbara's eyes met his. It was apparent in that look that this was one lady who was quite used to being in control of any and all situations. The shock was gone. So was the instant when she'd allowed her emotions to rule.

"Claire doesn't get paper cuts," she said.

"Maybe she was in a hurry to leave and cut herself on a suitcase. Maybe she nicked her shin when she shaved her legs," Dalton suggested. "There was no sign of any intruder, nothing in the house was disturbed and Ms. Jenkins had to disable the alarm."

Barbara fell into her seat, her brow wrinkled as she digested the information. Dalton used the silence to scan the wall behind her. It was a collage of awards, diplomas and glossy ads, all matted and professionally framed. The tributes spanned several years, telling him that her success had been earned.

"Then Claire must have been abducted by someone she knew."

Dalton sighed. "There is no indication that Ms. Benedict was abducted."

"The call to Haley and the blood aren't suspicious to you, Detective Ross?"

He offered a conciliatory nod. "A little. But without anything more to go on, I'm afraid there can be no formal investigation for another twenty-four hours."

The woman grunted and steepled her fingers as she leaned her elbows on the neatly arranged desk. "Try going on this," she began tersely. "Claire Benedict has a recently released felon for an ex-husband and a recently dumped boyfriend with a fatal-attraction thing going. Does that information make this a little more worthy of your time?"

Reaching into the pocket of his jacket, he pulled out a tattered notepad and then took one of the polished pens from the desk set and began writing. "What's the husband's name?"

"Ex-husband. Justin Benedict."

"What was he charged with?"

"He was *convicted* of embezzling funds from one of Claire's foundations."

"Foundations?"

Barbara's smile lacked mirth. "Claire Benedict has a net worth in the high seven figures. Family money."

Dalton nodded pensively. "And the boyfriend?"

"Ex-boyfriend. No one knows who he is. Claire was pretty secretive with us."

"Is that normal?"

Barbara shrugged. "If she thinks we'll tell her she's screwing up again, yes."

"Again?"

Barbara sighed. "Claire, Susan—"

"That would be Susan Taylor?"

Barbara nodded. "Claire, Susan, Haley and I have been friends since our tender years at the Sea Island Academy. Then it was off to Swiss boarding schools, summers traveling all over the world, anything that would save our parents from having to parent."

Dalton was having a hard time sympathizing with her perceived plight. "Is there a point?"

Barbara glared at him. "I see," she began evenly.

"Only the economically challenged are entitled to dysfunctional families?"

Dalton shifted his weight in the chair. "I didn't mean any offense."

"Sure you did. But to get back to your question, yes, there is a point. The four of us are very close. Whenever there's a problem, we share it."

"Is that why you don't know the name of this allegedly threatening boyfriend?"

Barbara gave him a small nod of surrender. "Claire's choices when it comes to men have always been less than prudent."

"Which means?"

"Justin was a loser looking for an easy way out of his work-study life at college. We all told Claire that he was trouble, but she convinced herself that if she loved Justin enough, he'd amount to something."

"Did he?"

Barbara made a derisive little sound. "After he married Claire, he dressed better. But that was about the extent of his transformation. Claire wouldn't listen to any of us when it came to Justin. But then, he always put his best foot forward when she was in earshot."

"So how'd he get convicted?"

"Haley."

Dalton found his interest piqued. "She prosecuted him?"

Barbara laughed. "Persecuted would be a better

word. Haley devised this rather elaborate plan, which resulted in getting enough evidence to convince Claire that Justin was screwing her in more than just the biblical sense.''

He felt the corners of his mouth tug into a smile. ''Should I ask how she accomplished this?''

''She broke into the foundation offices and copied all the financial records. Then she did some legal stuff and got the bank records. Needless to say, Justin's phony bookkeeping didn't hold up under an independent audit.''

''Justin was recently released from prison?''

''About two months ago. He called Claire when he got out and actually tried to convince her that his prison experience had changed him and he wanted a fresh start.''

''But Ms. Benedict wasn't impressed by his…freshness?''

Barbara laughed. ''She was already involved with the latest loser, so Justin got the brush-off.''

''The fatal-attraction mystery man?''

''If anyone hurt Claire, it was probably him.''

''Why?''

''Claire called me the night she threw him out.''

''He didn't take it well?''

''She called from the emergency room. The guy beat her to a pulp.''

''DON'T TELL ME you didn't notice that he's gorgeous,'' Barbara teased as she lifted the Scotch and water to her lips.

Haley refused to rise to the bait. "At the time, I was distracted by the blood in Claire's foyer."

Barbara's expression grew somber. "Sorry."

Haley glanced around the dining room of the Rose Tattoo. When her eyes found a familiar face, she groaned. "I just spent ten hours with him," she moaned. "I wish I'd never told Lawrence Betterman about this place."

Barbara turned her head as Haley continued to watch her boss elegantly glide up to a bar stool and hoist his trim body onto the seat. His age and attire made him look more than just a little out of place among the thirty-something crowd.

"Maybe he just comes here to sneak glances at you," Barbara suggested.

"Maybe I'll slit my wrists," Haley shot back with a chuckle. "He's everything I despise in the legal profession."

"Then why do you work for him?"

Haley shrugged. "They have to promote a woman to partner. The firm is getting a lot of heat from various groups. I've got a decent shot at it so long as I keep Betterman, Grimes, Kellerman and Phelps happy."

"Then why don't you mosey over there and invite him to join us?"

Haley sighed loudly. "I suppose I should. Good politics. But I'd really rather enjoy my drink."

"You'll never make partner with that attitude," Barbara warned.

"Right now I'm a little more concerned with Claire than I am about my career."

"Have you considered the possibility that she just took off?" Barbara suggested.

"Without telling any of us?" Haley argued. "Even if she did suddenly get a wild hare and decide to head for some tropical island, she would have called by now."

"The gorgeous detective doesn't think so."

Haley frowned at her friend. "Why do you say that?"

"Dark hair and broad shoulders. But mostly it's those bedroom eyes. The amber flecks really stand out with his dark lashes and tanned skin."

"Not that part," Haley said, sighing. "I meant why doesn't Detective Ross think Claire would contact us?"

Barbara shrugged. "He has already decided that we're a collection of spoiled women playing at life."

"Great," Haley grumbled. "Then why didn't you pull one of your famous Julia Sugarbaker impersonations and set him straight?"

"I thought I'd leave him for you," Barbara answered with a glint in her eyes. "He'd be a change of pace for you. The guy is definitely denim."

"Excuse me?"

"The men you usually date are cashmere. Detective Ross is definitely denim."

"I think you've been writing too many jeans ads," Haley groaned. "Besides, he wouldn't even make it onto my short list."

"Because he's a cop?"

"Right the first time. I don't do aggressive, dangerous men with handguns. Call me crazy, but I have this strange aversion to post-pubescents who run into dark alleys and use words like 'perp' and 'CI.'"

"What's a CI?"

"Confidential informant," Haley answered absently. Her attention was on Susan, who was standing next to Lawrence Betterman and having a very animated conversation. "Hey," she called to their waiter.

"Yes?"

"Could you send Susan over?"

He looked a little annoyed, but nodded.

"Why did you do that?" Barbara asked.

"Because I'll never make partner if Susan offers to come over to the offices to cleanse the place of negative energy."

"Good point," Barbara agreed. "She told me my commode was in the wrong place in my bathroom and suggested I put out a basket of daisy petals and hang a mirror on the door to deflect the bad vibes."

"Betterman will never take me seriously if he finds out Susan and I are friends."

"Betterman will probably have you committed when he learns your best buddy is a total fruit."

"Hi," Susan greeted cheerfully as she came up to the table. "I didn't know y'all were coming in tonight. Is there any word from Claire?"

Haley and Barbara shook their heads in unison. Haley spoke up. "No. And the detective said—"

"Who cares what he said," Susan interrupted. "With his looks who cares what comes out of his mouth?"

"Great," Haley grumbled. "I see Detective Ross has rendered you both temporarily insane."

"He'd be perfect for you," Susan babbled on, blissfully immune to Haley's cutting stare. "With your fair coloring and his brooding, dark masculinity, you'd have perfect yin and yang."

"My yin isn't the least bit impressed with his yang," Haley insisted. "And I hope you weren't discussing my karma with Mr. Betterman."

"Larry?" Susan asked.

"Larry?" Barbara parroted with a laugh. "I thought you said he went by Lawrence."

"He does," Haley said. Visions of her partnership vaporizing flashed through her mind. "Please tell me you didn't say anything about me."

"I told Larry we were friends. He seems really upset about Claire."

Haley frowned and glanced at the now vacant stool where Mr. Betterman had been seated. "How did he know about Claire?"

"He said you had mentioned it today."

Haley nodded, recalling then that Betterman had been in her office when she'd instructed her secretary to put through any call from Claire, regardless.

"You didn't say anything stupid to him, did you?" Barbara asked.

Susan pouted. "What is that supposed to mean?"

"You didn't suggest that he sniff cinnamon or boil a cup of vanilla to soothe the energy in his house, did you?"

"Ladies," Haley interrupted before the mood turned ugly. "I don't mean to be unkind, Susan, but I would feel better if you didn't share some of your more...eclectic leanings with my boss. I don't want him to think I'm anything but exceptional."

"He knows that," Susan said through a smile. "He says you're one of the brightest prospects at the firm."

Haley felt herself relax. "Let's keep it that way."

"I told the detective that Claire has not left town."

Haley looked up at Susan and gave her a warm smile. "I hope he listened to you. He seems to believe that she's just off soaking up the sun."

Susan shook her head. "He can't possibly believe that now. I told him that I could still feel Claire's energy, so she has to be in Charleston."

"You'll feel *my* energy if you don't get back to work."

The stern rebuke came from Rose Porter, proprietor of the Rose Tattoo. She placed her hand on Haley's shoulder as Susan fled. "How are you ladies tonight?"

"Worried about Claire," Haley answered.

"Some detective was here earlier," Rose said. "He was cute, Haley. Seemed like your type."

Barbara tried, unsuccessfully, to hide a laugh behind her hand. Haley rolled her eyes.

"What?" Rose demanded. "He was handsome. A hell of an improvement over those fancy sissy-boys you usually date."

"Thank you, Rose," Haley managed to say. "But I have a rule against dating cops."

"Rule, schmule," Rose scoffed. "When it comes to finding a man, you should depend on chemistry. It's like food, your body will let you know what it needs."

"Turn that into a cross-stitch sampler," Barbara joked.

Rose was about to comment further when she was called to another table. Her voice was as loud as her animal print shirt when she went into the kitchen and began chewing out the newest waitress for confusing orders.

"I'm going back to Claire's," Haley announced.

"To do what?" Barbara asked.

"Look around." Haley shrugged. "According to Detective Ross, there wasn't enough blood to even warrant a search by the crime scene people."

"Is that why you don't like him?"

Haley grunted in disgust as she rose, digging into her purse for a few bills in the process. "I'm not going to discuss Detective Ross. I never said I didn't like him, but unlike the rest of you, I'm focused."

"Frigid," Barbara countered in a stage whisper.

"ARE YOU SURE this is legal?" Barbara asked as they disarmed the alarm and went inside.

"I have keys and, according to the police, there is nothing mysterious about Claire's sudden disappearance. For all they care, I could be here to rob her blind."

Haley flipped a light switch and flooded the foyer with light.

"Those two little specks are what you got all fired up about?" Barbara asked.

Haley turned and glared at her friend. "Have you ever seen drops of blood on Claire's floor before?"

"Droplets," Barbara corrected. "Maybe Detective Gorgeous is right."

"Stop calling him that," Haley snapped. "If you're going to call him anything, try Detective Do-Nothing."

"I could arrest you."

Haley spun around to find the aforementioned detective framed in the doorway of Claire's living room.

"How did you get in here?" she demanded.

He offered her a sexy half smile that all but turned her legs to mush. Still, she managed to keep her composure as she looked up to meet his eyes.

"I had the alarm company give me the code. What about you?" he asked as he took two long strides toward her.

"I think I'll just step into the office," Barbara said. "I'm sure there are some plants that need watering in there."

"Traitor," Haley mumbled under her breath. "I'm here to look around," she told him with an intentionally challenging lift of her chin.

"This is a police matter, Ms. Jenkins."

"That doesn't seem to matter to the police, Detective."

His smile broadened. "You're quick, Counselor."

"I'm worried about my friend."

"And you think breaking and entering will help her?"

Haley almost bristled at the stern tone. Of course it wasn't half as distracting as feeling his warm breath against her cheek. Or the first whiff of his subtle, masculine cologne as he reached up and raked his fingers through his hair.

"I did no such thing," she said as she stiffened her spine. "I simply wanted to see if there was anything here in the house that could explain Claire's disappearance.''

"Maybe she left because she got cold feet."

"Cold feet about what?"

"Her...appointment with Dr. Dixon."

"What are you talking about?"

"She missed her appointment. I spoke with the good doctor this afternoon."

"That's impossible. Claire would not have missed that appointment for anything."

"So she was committed to buying an offspring?"

"What the hell is that supposed to mean?"

He made a rather derisive sound. "Your bored little rich friend decides to have a baby, so she buys one. That's pretty much what Dixon is selling."

"The last time I checked, Detective, Claire had a constitutional right to have a child. Has that changed?"

"No. I just have a problem with her means."

"Her means are none of your business," Haley defended. "So I guess you've decided that Claire isn't worthy of your investigating skills? Fine. Leave."

"I suppose that *you'll* do the same thing when you decide a child would be convenient?"

"This isn't about me, Detective. This is about Claire."

"Haley!" Barbara called from the office. "Come have a look at this."

Haley, with Dalton on her heels, raced into the office. They found Barbara standing over the fax machine, waiting for the printout to finish.

"What is it?"

"The journal," Barbara explained. "Claire received two faxes at around four-thirty yesterday."

"Wasn't her appointment with Dr. Dixon for four-forty-five?" the detective asked with a rather triumphant smirk.

Haley glared at him. "Dixon's clinic is a half mile from here. That doesn't prove a thing." Haley then told Barbara of the detective's claim that Claire had missed the long-awaited appointment. "Tell him how impossible that is," Haley prompted. "There's no way Claire would have missed seeing Dr. Dixon."

"Who are the faxes from?" he asked.

"No names, only numbers. One is out of state," Barbara supplied as she handed Dalton the journal page. "And I agree with Haley. Claire was more than committed to going through with the procedure."

"Is that what you ladies call conception?"

"What's with him?" Barbara asked.

"Apparently, aside from being an expert in criminology, the detective is also the moral guardian of society."

"Considering Claire's track record with men, artificial insemination was the only way to go. None of the men she dated came from a gene pool anyone should swim in.''

"Then why didn't she keep the appointment?''

"Simple,'' Haley answered. "Dr. Dixon has to be lying.''

"Not likely,'' he said, effectively dismissing her theory out of hand.

"Doctors don't lie?'' she countered smugly.

"Not this time. The doctor's story checks out.''

"Don't tell me one of his faithful nurses swears that her esteemed boss never saw Claire?''

"Actually—'' Dalton paused long enough to turn those unsettling hazel eyes on her ''—your esteemed boss was with him from four o'clock until they went out for dinner around seven.''

"*My* boss?'' Haley said in astonishment.

"Lawrence Betterman the Third.''

Chapter Three

Leaning back in his chair, Dalton laced his fingers behind his head and watched as Haley sauntered toward his office. His eyes studied the graceful way she seemed to glide through the chaos of the precinct. She didn't stop for directions, nor did she seem to notice the appreciative stares of the male officers. The women among the ranks appeared to regard her with a mixture of awe and envy. Too bad she was a lawyer.

She entered without knocking and closed the door with enough force to rattle the dented metal blinds that scraped the glass pane where his name had been painted a year earlier.

"You haven't returned my calls."

Unlacing his fingers, Dalton sighed and scooted his chair closer to his cluttered desk. "Nice to see you again, Ms. Jenkins."

Her frown did little to mar the extraordinary perfection of her features. She was one of those people who simply had to breathe to be beautiful. Her face was perfectly proportioned—big pale blue eyes, small straight nose, incredible lips and brilliant white teeth. The package was completed by a mane of wild, honey-colored curls that spilled well past her shoulders in no particular pattern. Dalton wondered if her hair was as soft and silky as it looked. What would she look like with all that hair fanned out on a pillow?

"Detective?" she prompted more forcefully. "You can forget it if you think I'll let you ignore me in person."

"That would be an accomplishment, Ms. Jenkins," he murmured as he pointed to one of the chairs opposite his desk. "Since you're here, why don't you have a seat?"

Her briefcase hit the floor with a dull thud but the woman lowered herself with the grace and elegance of royalty. The soft blue suit and dignified white blouse should have given her that frumpy professional-woman look. Instead, she looked feminine. Too damned feminine.

"What did you learn from the fax journals?"

He couldn't help but smile. "You aren't real big on pleasantries, are you?"

"I'm worried about Claire."

"Then I guess that means you haven't heard from her?"

"Would I be here if I had?"

Cocking his head to one side, Dalton purposefully broadened his smile. "Would you?"

The only indication that his mild flirtation had affected her was the tension in her hands. Her long, tapered fingers clenched the handle of her purse.

"Spare me the juvenile come-on, Detective. I want to know what progress you've made."

I made you flinch, he thought with satisfaction. Donning his most benign expression, Dalton looked down and shuffled through the stack of files on his desk. Pulling one from the stack, he flipped it open and took his time reading the typed report. He could feel her agitation and for some childish reason, he read the document a second time. Maybe he just liked the scent of her perfume. Maybe he just wanted to get even with her for her accurate call regarding his come-on. Maybe he just wanted this encounter to last. Dalton dismissed the last possibility in a flash as he snapped the file closed.

"The first fax came from a residence in Mt. Pleasant. The second was from a business in Maryland."

"Maryland?" Haley repeated. "Claire doesn't know anyone in Maryland."

"What about Mt. Pleasant?"

"I think that's where her ex-boyfriend lives. If you get the local usage for her telephone, I'm sure you can get the guy's name."

"If you four ladies were so tight, why didn't Claire tell you about her latest lover?"

"Ex-lover," Haley corrected. "The relationship only lasted about six weeks. I think there was violence early on. Claire was probably afraid we would start harping about her propensity toward treating men like projects."

"What does that mean?"

The small lines around her mouth relaxed slightly, as did the gentle slope of her shoulders. His gaze shifted to her hand as she twirled a long tendril of hair around one finger. It was the only sign of any nervousness.

"Claire believes that unconditional love can cure all."

Dalton added this information to the picture he'd been forming of the absent Miss Benedict. "And the rest of you don't?"

She looked at him through the veil of her lashes, her head tilted to one side, her expression mocking. "I can't speak for Barbara or Susan, but I don't think love can cure criminal behavior. I'll bet you don't either."

He couldn't help but grin at that. "Point. So Claire was into criminal types?"

"Claire had an ideal life," she began.

Dalton was trying his damnedest to listen to her words and not the sultry cadence of her unusually deep, seductive voice.

Haley continued. "She genuinely believed that all a jerk needed was the love of a good woman."

"You sound skeptical."

"Experienced."

That got his attention. "You don't impress me as the type to get…snookered."

Her eyes sparkled amusement at his word choice. "Only once. He was a cop."

Dalton almost winced. His intellect told him it was just as well. She might be drop-dead gorgeous, but she wasn't his type; he wasn't interested in her. Why, then, did her revelation sound like a gauntlet being thrown at his feet?

"Did you recover the faxes when you searched the house?" Haley pressed.

"We didn't search the house."

"What!"

"We can't even consider Ms. Benedict as officially missing until tonight at midnight," he explained. "She's an adult."

Haley got to her feet, glaring at him as she retrieved her briefcase. "I thought you were taking this seriously."

"I am."

"Then why aren't you doing something?"

"Look," he began, matching her tone and volume, thereby earning some pointed stares from his colleagues. "I've already broken departmental guidelines by conducting some preliminary interviews. Anything else will have to wait until an official investigation is deemed warranted."

"Nicely memorized, detective," Haley snapped, seething. "If anything happens to Claire, I'll hold you personally responsible."

"You can go in now."

Haley nodded to Mr. Betterman's secretary before smoothing the front of her skirt and walking across the thick plush carpet. She took a deep breath before opening the door to what the associates called the Inner Sanctum. It was actually the executive conference room where the senior partners gathered to do whatever it was they did when they weren't dictating performance memos or wining and dining potential clients.

Lawrence Betterman III was seated at the far end of the table. He didn't even lift his head as she quietly closed the door. Surprisingly, Jonathan Phelps was there as well, standing next to the bar mixing himself a drink. Mr. Phelps turned his balding head and gave her a warm smile. She returned the gesture, noting that even the two-thousand-dollar suit didn't make him look any less like the nerdy tax attorney he was.

Betterman was a different story. He looked like one of those celebrity attorneys. Elegantly tailored suits and flamboyant ties. Dark brown hair perfectly coiffed and plastered into place with hair spray. His persona was completed with a daily buffing and manicure of his nails. His only visible flaw was a small bandage on his pinkie finger.

"Can I get you something, Ms. Jenkins?" Phelps asked.

"No, thank you. I'd like to speak to you, Mr. Betterman. It's a personal matter."

Betterman looked up, but not at her. Instead his gaze went to Phelps. "I believe she wishes to discuss the matter of her friend's missed appointment with Michael Dixon."

Haley stood perfectly still, trying to figure out what was going on.

Betterman saved her the trouble. When he finally deigned to look in her general direction, his expression wasn't exactly friendly. "I don't appreciate having a police detective questioning me."

Haley swallowed. "I'm sure he was just doing his job."

Betterman continued to stare at her. "I understand that you were the one who reported this Benedict woman missing?"

"She's a very close friend," Haley explained. "And this firm handles the legal work for her various trusts," she added, praying Betterman's attitude would improve.

Betterman looked to Phelps, who nodded before opening his mouth to speak.

"We realize substantial earnings from the Benedict holdings," Phelps explained. Then, smiling at

Haley, he added, "Miss Jenkins brought her to the firm shortly after she was hired."

Betterman's whole demeanor had her seething internally. Obviously Claire was nothing more than billable hours to this man. Lord, he was an uncaring jerk.

"Then it would seem your actions were prudent," Betterman pronounced as if from on high. "I trust the outcome will be positive."

Haley counted to ten slowly. The man was heartless and, apparently, tactless. She was about to remind him that Claire Benedict wasn't an outcome, she was a human being. The instant her lips separated, Phelps grasped her elbow and guided her from the room.

Once they were out of earshot of Betterman's secretary, he led Haley to an alcove near the water cooler. "I hope you know how concerned we all are."

"Mr. Betterman didn't exactly give me that impression," Haley said, choosing her words carefully.

Mr. Phelps gave her a weak smile. "Lawrence can be harsh at times. You have my assurance that he's concerned."

"Concerned about what?" Haley asked.

"Well," Phelps's Adam's apple bobbed above the too-tight collar of his white shirt. "We can't have the police coming here to interrogate the senior partner. And then there's the matter of your performance."

"Excuse me?"

"The Mulhulland case?"

Haley closed her eyes and leaned against the wall. "I forgot he was coming in this afternoon."

"Apparently," Mr. Phelps agreed with a tinge of sadness in his voice. "I know your friend's disappearance is upsetting to you, but the Mulhulland divorce is complicated. Mr. Mulhulland was quite upset when you missed the meeting."

"I'll go and call him," Haley promised. "I'll arrange another meeting at his convenience. It won't happen again."

"I'm sure it won't," Phelps replied, though there was a subtle threat behind the statement. "You've done some exceptional work here, Miss Jenkins. Partnership considerations are only a month away. It isn't prudent for you to become lax in your work at this juncture."

"No, sir."

"Then I would suggest you keep your personal life out of this office."

"I will," Haley promised.

A few minutes later she was safely locked in her office, massaging her temples and silently cursing herself. Mulhulland was a personal friend of Betterman's and she had missed an important meeting regarding the upcoming deposition. At least she now understood why Betterman had been so distant during her audience.

It took her a full five minutes to work up the cour-

age to place the call to Mulhulland. His secretary left
her on hold for a few minutes before putting her
through.

"This is Haley Jenkins," she said quickly. "I'm
calling to apologize for this afternoon and to resched-
ule our appointment."

"Where the hell were you?" Mulhulland growled.
"Do you have any idea how hard it is for me to get
away from here? It puts my whole operation at risk."

She wanted to tell him that she didn't give a fig,
but that wasn't an option. She also wanted to point
out that he sold used luxury automobiles, not defense
satellites, but that wasn't an option either.

"I can only repeat my apology, Mr. Mulhulland.
If you'll just tell me what would be convenient for
you, I'll rearrange my schedule to accommodate
whatever you need."

"That's more like it," he conceded.

She could almost see his barrel chest puffing out
with self-importance.

"First Lawrence, then you. I was beginning to
wonder what kind of operation y'all had going down
there."

Obviously Mulhulland still hadn't gotten over the
fact that Betterman had assigned his nasty divorce to
a lowly associate instead of handling it himself.

It took two more minutes of listening to Mulhulland vent before they agreed to a time late the
following week. As Haley placed the phone on the
cradle, she closed her eyes and silently prayed that

she would see Claire long before she would see Mr. Mulhulland and his tiger's-head pinkie ring with the fake ruby eyes.

Calls to Barbara and Susan proved fruitless—still no word from Claire. Haley found it impossible to think of Claire without thinking about Dalton Ross. Why did he have to be a cop?

Roxanne, her secretary, stuck her head in the door to say good-night. Haley didn't need to check the wall clock. Roxanne left at precisely five every day. If the workload was heavy, Roxanne would come in early, but she had to leave at the stroke of five. Her young son had to be picked up from the day care center, no exceptions.

Turning to her computer terminal, Haley typed in the code that allowed her to pull up the client database. The system was designed so that any attorney could access the firm's client list. The purpose was to make sure that there was never a conflict of interest in the firm. Everything was cross-referenced just to make certain. She typed in *Michael Dixon, M.D.* Frowning, she tried typing it without the M.D., but got the same result. Dixon was a client. But his counsel of record wasn't Lawrence Betterman, it was Jonathan Phelps.

"So why," Haley murmured to the screen, "were you having dinner with good ol' Larry?"

Chapter Four

Haley stumbled over the hem of her robe as she raced down the darkened stairs while trying to tie her belt. At the bottom of the steps, she hit her toe against something hard and metal. Tears welled in her eyes as an expletive fell past her lips.

She punched the light switch, remembering too late that Malcolm the contractor and his Merry Men had cut the breaker to this part of the house.

"Yes?" she called through the door.

"It's midnight."

She hated the way her heart fluttered at the sound of his voice. Raking her disheveled hair out of her eyes, she yanked open the door and glared up at his silhouette. "So what are you doing here?"

Dalton stepped inside, brushing her body as he passed. The strength and warmth of his large frame didn't go unnoticed. Haley struggled to will her hormones into submission.

"Forget to pay your light bill?"

Following the scent of his cologne, she trailed after him as he moved almost silently down the narrow hallway. "Partial darkness is my latest gift from Malcolm. What are you doing here?"

"Investigating. Who's Malcolm?"

"The general contractor from hell," she grumbled at his broad back. "Watch to the left up ahead, he's got trim stacked against the wall."

When they reached the archway that led into the kitchen, Haley had no choice but to step around him in order to reach the light. In that brief second when her body was close to his, she could feel the energy and power emanating from him. He seemed larger somehow. Larger and more dangerous.

It only got worse when the light came on and she caught her first real look at him. His shoulders fairly filled the narrow passageway. He was wearing the same gray shirt he'd had on that afternoon, only now the tie was gone and the top few buttons were open, displaying deeply tanned skin and a hint of the soft black hair that probably tapered down to his trim waist. Haley felt her internal temperature rise as she created a picture in her mind of what he might look like beneath his slightly rumpled clothing. The shadow of a beard added a sexy, masculine appearance to a face that needed no such assistance. In fact, the man exuded a kind of primal sensuality that her own body seemed incapable of resisting.

"You're staring, Ms. Jenkins," he teased as he flashed a grin.

Tugging the edges of her robe together, Haley cleared her throat and quietly commanded herself to meet his eyes. "I'm just astonished to see you here."

"You are the same woman who reamed me this afternoon and threatened to hold me responsible if I didn't investigate, right?"

"So why are you here instead of out investigating?"

"Background," he said with a shrug of his shoulders. "Got any coffee?"

"Yes." Haley didn't move. She stood paralyzed with fascination as his eyes glided over her body, taking in every detail. Finally, she summoned the courage to say, "The coffee's in the freezer, the pot's on the counter. You can make it while I get dressed."

"Don't bother on my account," he murmured with an obscenely innocent expression.

Before the heat on her face turned into a flaming red blush, Haley was chased from the room by his low chuckle. Damn him!

DALTON WAS STILL STARING at the machine when she returned a few minutes later. He almost laughed when he saw her choice of clothing. The baggy T-shirt and even baggier jeans hid her impressive figure, but it was a wasted effort. His mind had already memorized every curve of her shapely body.

In fact, his brain had gone a step farther to imagine what she might look like wearing nothing but that infrequent smile of hers.

"I thought you were in charge of coffee," she said without making eye contact.

"I would be if you had a normal coffeepot."

"It happens to be top of the line," she returned haughtily. "It makes everything from espresso to cappuccino."

"How about good old regular?"

She came up next to him and practically ripped the bag of coffee from his hand. He didn't mind; it gave him an opportunity to be close to her. He could sense her tension as she set about the task of filling the basket with coffee. Her movements were stiff and there was just the slightest tremble in her hands. His male ego liked the fact that she wasn't as immune to him as she pretended. Not that he was interested in her. He couldn't have cared less that she smelled of flowers. It didn't matter that she looked sexy as hell with her hair all tousled as if she'd just been...

"Would you?"

"Would I what?"

"Move so that I can get to the sink?"

He did, but only fractionally. For some perverse reason known only to the testosterone that had taken control of his judgment, Dalton wasn't in any mood to put any distance between them.

When she reached over to turn on the faucet, her

forearm brushed his waist. It was like getting hit with a stun gun. Even through his shirt, his body held the electrifying surge from the brief encounter. He decided then that he was losing his mind. He hadn't reacted this way to a woman since his high school days. He didn't like the feeling. Damn her!

Going for safety, Dalton moved around the room, studying the furniture and other objects with mild interest. The house was a total disaster, unless you were one of those types who liked pouring money into a lost cause.

"Ms. Benedict saves men and you save houses?" he asked as he reached out to finger the paint samples on the kitchen table.

She stood with her back against the counter and watched him with wary eyes. "My legacy, I'm afraid."

"Buy cheap, renovate and sell high?"

That earned him a smile. A real one, a genuine one. Not those practiced fake ones she had tossed at him in the past. She was incredible when she smiled.

"This house has been in my family since the early nineteenth century. No one's lived here for decades. My parents preferred to live on the ocean, so they maintained the exterior to keep the Historic Societies at bay. The inside is a mess, so after my parents died, when I needed something to keep me busy, I decided to restore the place."

"What about practicing law?"

She poured two mugs of coffee before joining him at the round oak table that was probably an antique. Pricey or not, Dalton found the chairs cold and uncomfortable.

"I can do two things at once."

"I'm sure you can," he agreed as he purposefully brushed his fingers across hers as she handed him the mug. He watched her eyes when he touched her. Then he silently berated himself for trying so hard to get a rise out of this woman. He was being an ass.

"Are you here to investigate, Detective? Or were you hoping for a quick tumble?"

He winced and sucked in a breath. "I guess I deserved that. Sorry." He met her cool gaze and felt genuinely contrite. "I don't suppose you'd believe me if I told you that I don't make a habit of coming on to women."

"Not a chance."

He respected her honesty. "I could tell you that I'm simply rendered stupid by your looks. But I doubt that's very original."

"Why don't you just try acting professionally," Haley suggested in a perfect courtroom voice. "I can assure you that I'm not interested in you."

"I tell you you're beautiful and you take aim at my ego."

"I'm sure your ego can handle it."

Dalton shook his head and took a sip of the coffee. It was rich and hot and nothing like the tar he was used to down at the station. "If you'll overlook my behavior during the past few minutes, I promise to be a good boy from here on in."

She didn't respond right away. Instead, she tucked one bare foot beneath her as she shifted in her seat. Twirling a tendril of hair around her finger, she regarded him for what felt like an eternity. "Detective, I—"

"Dalton."

"Detective," she began more forcefully, "I doubt you've been a good boy for years. But I really don't care. What I want is your promise that you'll do everything possible to find Claire."

"Deal."

"Okay, so what do you do first?"

"Background. I need to rule out the possibility that she's absented herself by choice."

"She hasn't. Claire is one of those people who does everything by committee. She didn't even make her final decision about having the baby without talking it over with everyone in Charleston."

"Besides you, Susan and Barbara, who else does she talk to?"

"Her doctor."

"Dixon?"

Haley shook her head. "Dr. Tate, he's her regular ob/gyn. I know she spoke to Shelby, since Shelby was a single mom for a while."

"Shelby?"

"Tanner. She owns the Rose Tattoo on East Bay. Shelby and her partner, Rose Porter. I think Claire might have talked to them. But I think you should be looking at Justin, or even more likely, her last boyfriend."

"I'm seeing Justin tomorrow and if the records division comes through at the phone company, I'll start tracking down the boyfriend."

He watched as Haley rubbed her bare arms as if the mere mention of the men in Claire's life gave her a chill. That small display of vulnerability pulled at him in a way he didn't want to be pulled.

"If her ex-boyfriend is involved, Claire could be... He beat her," she added in a barely audible voice. "I've seen what he's capable of."

It only got worse when he watched the slight quiver of her bottom lip. He knew he had lost the battle when he saw her big blue eyes fill with unshed tears.

Slowly, he moved and went to her, carefully lifting her out of the chair and holding her against him. Her small hands gathered fistfuls of his shirt as her head fell against his chest. Awkwardly, he tentatively touched her back, careful to keep from putting his hands where they shouldn't be.

Haley was a good head shorter and her small frame made her seem all the more in need of comfort. But Dalton knew somewhere in the deepest part of his mind that he wanted to give her more than just comfort.

What kind of creep was he? The woman was soundlessly weeping and all he could think about was lifting her face to his and kissing her tears away. Hell, he wanted to do more than just kiss her tears. He wanted...

The shrill sound of the telephone sent Haley flying from his embrace. Swiping the tears from her cheeks, she grabbed the phone and he watched her expression change instantly.

Both hands gripped the receiver as she screamed, "Claire? Where are you? We've been frantic. I'm with the police now."

There was a short pause, then Haley's brows drew together. "You don't sound right. What's wrong and where are you?"

There was another pause. Dalton used this opportunity to go over to where Haley stood shaking. He reached out and tilted the receiver as he bent his head next to hers to listen.

"I'll meet you tomorrow," came the slurred female voice. "Tell the police it was nothing."

"You sound drunk, Claire. Tell me what's wrong?" Haley pleaded.

"Not drunk," came the answer. "In the morning, Haley. Just you and I'll explain everything. Meet me at Battery Park at seven."

"Claire!" Haley yelled, frustration evident in her frantic tone.

"Forget it," he said gently as he took the phone from her and placed it on the cradle. "She sounded like she was in the bag."

Haley tossed some of her hair over her shoulder and looked up into his eyes. "Claire never drinks. Ever. She is the ultimate fitness freak. No alcohol, no red meat. No exceptions."

"Everyone has an off day," Dalton tried.

"Look," Haley said as she backed away from him. "I guess Claire's call gets you off the hook."

Dalton wondered which one of them she was trying to convince. "I guess so."

"You'd better go."

"Will you do me a favor?"

Haley looked at him with caution clouding her eyes. "I suppose I owe you a favor after I cried all over your shirt."

Dalton grinned down at her. "Call me after you meet Claire. Just so I can put something in my file to keep the brass happy."

She nodded and Dalton couldn't think of anything else to say. He left her house with a mixture of regret and a cop's nagging intuition as companions. It just didn't feel right.

WITH HER BRIEFCASE in one hand and a cup of coffee in the other, Haley got to Battery Park just before seven. Her tired eyes burned in the bright August sunlight. The heat was already oppressive and lack of sleep didn't have her in the best of moods. She had replayed the phone call endlessly in her mind. It didn't make any sense. Maybe Claire was ill. That would explain the slurred speech and the spacey tone.

Selecting a conspicuous spot by the railing at the edge of the path, she looked out on the harbor at the empty slips of the shrimp boats, which had left hours earlier. The park was deserted save for the small contingent of roller-bladers, joggers and cyclists getting in their exercise before the temperature topped the hundred-degree mark.

Haley checked her watch. It was a few minutes after seven. She glanced around the park but saw no sign of Claire. She turned back and lifted the plastic-foam cup to her lips. The sound of an approaching cyclist reached her ears at almost the same instant she felt the burning pain between her shoulders.

Haley felt herself slumping forward against the railing, dropping the coffee and her briefcase in the process. It hurt to breathe. She reached behind her and felt for the source of the pain. Her fingers ran along the hilt of a knife and she heard a woman's scream. The scream, she realized, was her own.

Chapter Five

Dalton sprinted out from behind the massive trunk of a live oak, hurdling benches as he called her name. By the time he reached Haley, she lay crumpled in the grass, one hand grasping the railing, the other groping the knife handle.

"It's okay," Dalton said as he knelt and gently pulled her against his legs, careful not to make her injury worse. Cupping her head in his hand, he reached into his jacket and pulled out his cell phone. After flipping it open, he used his thumbnail to phone the dispatcher.

Haley looked up at him with wide, terrified eyes as he called for a marked unit and an ambulance. His heart was pounding in his chest as he spoke. "The suspect is on a bike. Black hooded sweatsuit, last seen exiting Battery Park at the corner of Water Street."

"What happened?"

A wave of relief washed over him when he heard

Haley speak. That meant the knife hadn't pierced a lung. "Don't try to talk," he said as he shrugged off his jacket and placed it over her. "The ambulance will be here in a few minutes."

Dalton brushed a few strands of hair off her face as he continued to hold her shivering body as close as possible. "Tough way to start the day," he teased, hoping to keep her from going into shock. Her face was white.

"What were you doing here?" she asked.

"Watching out for you," he answered honestly. "I won't get any medals for my performance, though."

"It wasn't—"

Haley didn't have an opportunity to finish the sentence. A team of paramedics pushed through the small crowd of gawkers and brushed Dalton aside. As much as he wanted to hold her hand, offer her some sort of reassurance, he knew she needed medical attention more than she needed his act of penance.

He barked commands to several uniformed officers before jogging back to his car to follow Haley to the hospital. Why the hell had he parked so far away? And why hadn't he positioned himself close enough to prevent her from being stabbed? "Why was she stabbed at all?" he murmured as he reached his car.

"YOU REALLY SHOULD be resting, Miss Jenkins," the nurse chided as she looked around the hospital room and found no fewer than three people in attendance. With a pointed glare at Rose, Susan and Dalton, she added, "The doctor should be in with your discharge papers and a prescription in just a few minutes."

"I've been resting for two days," Haley told the woman. "I'm ready for a little company." Her last remark was directed at Dalton and he didn't even flinch at her unspoken accusation. He'd ordered a twenty-four-hour guard at her door and no visitors had been allowed in. Not even Barbara.

The nurse made a disapproving noise as she swished from the room on her rubber-soled shoes. Dalton was leaning against the far wall, his expression nothing more than a hard mask. Susan was clutching some sort of crystal and mumbling an incantation that she had assured Haley would rid her of the memory of the traumatic event. Rose was seated in the cracked-vinyl chair, her attention seeming to volley between Haley and Dalton.

"Why did you think it was necessary to keep us out?" Rose demanded of the stoic figure. "If anyone should have been kept away, it was you. You sat back on your heels while that lunatic stabbed her."

"Rose," Haley began in a placating tone, "I'm sure the detective would have done something if he could have."

"You should have shot the son of a—"

"Rose!" Haley said sharply. "It happened too fast."

Patting her teased and lacquered hair, Rose refused to give up. She offered Dalton one of her most withering looks before she said, "Susan, go bring the car around front. I'm sure Haley wants to leave as soon as the doctor gives his okay."

"I'm taking her home," Dalton announced.

"That isn't n-necessary," Haley stammered, surprised by his pronouncement. "Rose has been kind enough to give Susan the day off. Barbara's coming over after work. I won't be alone."

Dalton turned his hazel eyes on her and without moving, repeated calmly, "I'm taking you home."

"Is your interest personal or professional?"

"Rose!" Haley yelped as she felt her face flame. "You don't have to dignify that with an answer," she assured Dalton.

"Thanks, Counselor," he quipped.

"Yes, he does," Rose insisted.

"Not again, Rose," Susan wailed. "You promised you would stop interfering in other people's lives."

"I'm not interfering."

"You're embarrassing me," Haley said. "He can take me home."

The slight nod of Dalton's head in response allowed a single lock of dark hair to fall against his forehead. It gave him an earthy, slightly mussed appearance that made Haley silently grateful for the fact that her pulse rate was no longer being monitored by a machine.

"What about me?" Susan cried. "Rose said I could have the day off to look after you."

Rose stood and took Susan's wrist. "I have a feeling the detective will be doing enough looking for the both of you."

Haley's blush got even worse as the door closed after Rose and Susan and she found herself alone with him. The room seemed suddenly small and the air filled with her tightly coiled anticipation. She studied the edge of the bed where her fingers gripped the mattress. Her feet didn't touch the floor, making her feel vulnerable. The fact that Susan had selected her most hideous dress and her oldest sandals didn't help much. And this was definitely the ultimate in bad hair days.

She was glad there wasn't a mirror in the room. She didn't want to know what she looked like after two days in a hospital bed with no makeup and her arm in a sling.

"Does it hurt?"

Haley shrugged, then winced. "Only when I do that."

"Then don't do that," he teased. Dalton stepped closer, standing just in front of her. His hand reached out and he caught her chin with his thumb and forefinger. Tilting her face to his, he studied her eyes. "Seriously, how do you feel?"

"About as good as I look."

His lopsided grin and the feel of his callused fingers against her skin caused a shiver to run through her. Her nails dug into the mattress as she fought the urge to touch his hand.

"Why are you doing this?" she asked. "I understand the guard, but I don't know why you're acting like a chauffeur. That isn't part of the job description."

His hand fell away, dropping to his side. "You're wrong, Haley. It is my job to make sure you're safe."

So this was all about him just doing his job? That explained why he hadn't once visited her in the hospital. The knowledge should have made her happy, or at the very least relieved. Her one experience with a cop had ended with a funeral. She could never be happy with Dalton. It was just as well that his interest was purely professional.

Then why do I feel so disappointed?

"WHAT DO YOU MEAN we aren't staying here?"

"I want you to pack whatever you need. You're a sitting duck in this house."

Haley resisted the childish urge to rip her elbow out of his hand as they climbed the front steps to her house. The sounds of hammering, sawing and the blare of country music pounded out from the opened windows.

"How are you supposed to rest with all this going on?" Dalton argued as he opened the door.

"I'm used to it," she yelled above the noise. "Besides, with Malcolm and his men here, I'm perfectly safe."

As if on cue, Malcolm appeared in the hallway, an unlit cigarette dangling from the corner of his mouth. One bushy eyebrow rose as he looked from Haley to Dalton, then back to her. "How you doin'?"

"I'm fine," she answered as a few of the workmen stopped their respective tasks to give her a once-over. "Could someone turn down the music?"

"Junior!" Malcolm yelled. "Shut off the radio!"

"Thanks."

"TV said you was mugged in the park," Malcolm commented.

Haley looked up at Dalton, who warned her with his eyes. "The TV never lies," she offered with a forced smile.

"I want you and your crew to take the rest of the day off," Dalton announced.

Haley was about to contradict him when she felt the tight squeeze of his fingers on her arm. "The doctor said I should rest," she said to Malcolm.

"It's gonna cost," he said with a shrug of his shoulders. The action exposed a fair amount of his rounded stomach and huge silver belt buckle, which was crafted in the shape of a hammer.

Haley nodded and sighed. "It always does."

Malcolm and his men cleared out while Haley showered. The few minutes of solitude were a welcome relief from the past few days of being monitored every four hours by the hospital staff.

"Who are you kidding?" she asked her reflection as she carefully blotted the line of stitches. "You're hiding up here."

"Hiding from what?"

Clutching the towel around her, Haley leaned against the closed bathroom door and yelled, "What are you doing up here?"

"I came up to help you rebandage your wound."

"When pigs fly!"

She could hear his deep, throaty chuckle through the door.

"C'mon, Haley. You have to keep it covered. You don't want any infections now, do you?"

She hadn't really thought about that. "I can do it myself," she called out. "But thanks anyway."

Closing her eyes, she listened for sounds of his footsteps. Nothing. "I said I could take care of it."

"I know what you said," he answered in a reasonable tone. "I think you're acting like a child. What do you think I'll do? You've got a dozen stitches on your back."

He's not interested in you. He said so at the hospital. I can't reach to put the bandage on, so it makes perfect sense to let him do it.

"Just a second," she called through the door.

Haley searched the room for options. Finally, she settled on wrapping a towel around her, then putting her robe loosely over the towel. She didn't open the door until she had a second towel in her hand, just in case anything slipped.

Dalton looked completely relaxed and at home with his hands full of gauze pads and adhesive tape. Haley swallowed, she didn't dare meet his eyes. He might be relaxed but she was one giant, vibrating nerve. Maybe it was simple exhaustion. Maybe it was leftover jitters from the attack. Maybe it was having this gorgeous man standing in her bedroom.

ACT CASUAL, he repeated to himself as he watched her emerge. As she passed, he could smell the floral freshness of her shampoo. Her damp hair had been combed, making it appear darker as the unruly curls framed her oval face. It was a genuine struggle to keep his body from reacting to her.

"Sit on the bed," he instructed.

Clutching the towel against her chest, Haley stiffly followed his instruction. She wouldn't even look at him as he leaned on one knee and positioned himself behind her. Dalton put the bandages on the bed and lifted her hair off her back, draping it forward over her shoulder. When his knuckles brushed the silky skin at her neck, he almost groaned. Haley wasn't making it any easier. He heard the small intake of her breath when he touched her. His intellect told him it was a normal reaction. His libido had a completely different interpretation. Did she make those little noises when she made love?

Dalton fairly yanked the terry-cloth robe as he silently berated himself for his thoughts. The small wound did nothing to mar the absolute perfection he saw before him. Though it wasn't necessary, he tugged the robe almost to her waist, taking the damp towel down as well. The graceful way her spine divided her body into perfect halves was nearly his undoing. Her body was perfect. Too perfect.

Biting his lower lip, Dalton quickly got the gauze into place. It wasn't until he rearranged her clothing that he dared to breathe again. "I'll get your sling."

"No way," Haley answered with her back to him. "It doesn't do much good and it's hot and uncomfortable."

He watched her as she went to a large wardrobe and used only one arm to open each door. "The doctor said you should use it for a few days."

Her back was still to him. "The doctor won't know."

Dalton rolled his eyes. "I might call him when we get to the safe house."

Twirling on her bare feet, Haley nearly fell when the towel slipped from beneath her robe. She cursed softly, then kicked the towel across the floor before her sparkling blue eyes dared him to laugh. "I'm not going anywhere. I'm staying right here."

With the heels of his hands, he pressed against his eyes and summoned an extra dose of patience. "You can't stay here. This house can't be secured."

"Secured from what?"

Dalton saw Barbara just a split second before the redhead appeared in the doorway. "This is exactly what I'm talking about," he said with a sigh.

"Hello to you too," Barbara tossed back at him. "How are you feeling?" she said as she went over and gave Haley one of those air kisses that were a trademark among the rich and spoiled.

"I'll be fine as soon as I'm allowed some peace and quiet."

"You won't be fine until we have Claire Benedict in custody."

Haley gaped at Dalton. "What are you talking about?" she demanded.

"You're a bright woman, Haley. Put it together. Claire arranges to meet you and you end up with a knife in the back."

"You can't possibly believe that Claire had anything to do with what happened in the park," she insisted rather loudly. "Tell him, Barbara."

The redhead lifted her shoulders and blew out a long breath. "It does seem a little too coincidental."

"Good grief, Barbara! You can't possibly think Claire would hurt me."

"I don't think she would, but that doesn't mean she isn't involved."

"Thank you," Dalton said. "Now, help me convince her to leave this house so my department can provide appropriate protection."

"Hold on," Haley said through tightly clenched teeth. "The two of you have lost your minds if you think I'm going to buy into your ludicrous notion that Claire is behind this. Haven't either of you ever heard the expression 'random act of violence'?"

"I saw it, Haley," Dalton fired back. "That was a well-planned, well-executed attack. The only people who knew you would be in the park that morning were Claire and me."

"Fat lot of good *you* were, too," Haley lashed back. "You stood there playing voyeur when that maniac stabbed me."

Dalton's jaw actually hurt from the struggle to keep his often-rehearsed defense to himself. He had wondered how long it would be before she got around to telling him what she really thought. That was the reason he hadn't mustered the guts to see her in the hospital. It was the reason he was going to find the guy himself.

"Haley," Barbara began in a placating tone, "he couldn't have known Claire was setting you up."

"Claire didn't set this up and you know that."

"Maybe," Barbara conceded, "but what about her loser boyfriend? You know how easily Claire can be conned."

At that instant both women looked to Dalton.

"Have you found him?" Haley asked.

"We got a name from running her phone usage records."

"And?" Haley demanded.

"And the guy hasn't been seen at his apartment since the night Claire disappeared."

He watched the play of emotions on Haley's face. They ranged from surprise to just a hint of fear. "So trace him through his driver's license. He must have convinced Claire to contact me, then he showed up instead."

"Why?" Dalton asked as he held her gaze.

"Because he's a violent jerk," Haley explained.

"Maybe, but that doesn't tell me why he would suddenly try to kill you. You told me you'd never met the guy—didn't even know his name."

"I don't," Haley assured him. "Claire could have told him I was helping her get a restraining order."

"But if she's with this guy willingly, why would he need to hurt you?"

Haley opened her mouth, then closed it. Her brows drew together as she apparently pondered the holes in her theory.

"What about Justin?" Barbara asked. "He has always believed that it was Haley's fault that he ended up in jail."

Raking his hair off his forehead, Dalton looked at Haley. "Justin is..."

"What?" Haley just about shouted. "Justin is what?"

"Missing."

Chapter Six

"You'd think he'd feel like a fool," Barbara commented.

Haley watched Betterman's reflection in the mirror above the massive fireplace that dominated one wall of the Rose Tattoo. "He does seem to have a real thing for young women. Every time he comes in here, he leaves with something young and stupid on his sleeve. No wonder his wife left him."

"Speaking of which, how did you get out from under the watchful bedroom eyes of Detective Ross?"

Letting out a long sigh, Haley took her fork and pushed a chunk of chicken around on her plate. "We've been avoiding each other."

"You must have suffered brain damage," Barbara quipped. "You don't avoid a man like him, not if you're normal."

Haley gave her friend a pointed glare. "I'm normal, I just refuse to even consider a man like Dalton.''

Barbara's smile was smug, knowing, and made Haley intensely irritable.

"Dalton?'' her friend purred. "That's a good sign. I have a bet with my assistant that the two of you will be together within a month.''

"Your assistant? Why would she care? And why would you be telling her about him in the first place?''

"She saw him the day he came to my office. She's already offered to have his child if you don't start dating him.''

"I won't date him, Barbara. He's not the kind of man I would even consider spending the rest of my life with.''

Barbara rolled her eyes. "I'm talking about a few dates and some meaningless sex. You don't have to marry him just because you've slept with him. You aren't Elizabeth Taylor.''

Haley laughed. "I'll give you that, but he's still not appropriate.''

Barbara's expression grew solemn. "Is all this resistance because of what happened with Cal?''

"That was a long time ago,'' Haley hedged.

"My point exactly.''

"Meaning?''

"I was sad when Cal was killed. He was a young rookie cop with a gung-ho attitude. Dalton has been a cop for almost twenty years. You can't compare the two.''

"It's the same job," Haley argued. "There's no guarantee that Dalton won't get careless the way Cal did." Haley put her fork down, leaving her chicken salad only half-eaten. Again her eyes went to the mirror, watching as the senior partner of her firm placed a couple of bills on the bar before he offered his arm to a fresh-faced brunette. "Betterman has a more active social life than I do. That's really sick."

"Your social life would be great if you'd just go home tonight and rip Dalton's clothes off."

"Get real." Haley sighed. "Besides, don't you get the impression that he's pretending?"

"Pretending?"

"He says the right things, apologizes when he comes on to me, but I get the feeling it's all some sort of front. The guy is probably as randy as a stray hound."

"Back up," Barbara said excitedly. "He's been coming on to you?"

"One time. He shot, he didn't score."

"You're hopeless," Barbara declared as she shook her fork like an angry finger. "Has it dawned on you that you're letting a ten-year-old memory haunt you?"

"Please," Haley groaned. "You make it sound like I crawled into the grave with Cal. You know perfectly well that I've dated a lot of men since then.''

"What I know is that you loved Cal when you were an idealistic twenty-five-year old. Memories have a way of sanitizing reality."

"I haven't sanitized anything."

"I was there, Haley," Barbara said. "You were just finishing law school and Cal had just graduated from the academy. He was a nice guy, but do you really think the two of you would have lasted if he hadn't been killed?''

"I'll never know."

"You should. As much as you might want to remember him in a positive light, I remember all the fights and the way he was so threatened by your career aspirations. If he was still alive, do you think he'd support your year-long push for a partnership? Do you think Cal would have been content with you working seventy-hour weeks?''

"This is a pointless conversation," Haley insisted. "I don't compare Dalton and Cal, so I don't think there's any reason you should."

"Right. And you ran away from home tonight because...?''

"I didn't run away from home," Haley insisted, though she felt compelled to lower her gaze as she said the words. "I'm going back to work tomorrow. I just wanted to talk to you about Claire."

"Has there been any word yet?"

Haley looked up to find Shelby Tanner standing at their table. Shelby could have been the poster child for Southern beauty and gentility. She was a tall, willowy brunette with a soft voice and a strong character. She was having an incredible hair day, too. As usual.

"Nothing yet," Haley answered. "The police think she's responsible for what happened in the park."

Shelby's dark brows drew together. "What do you think?"

"I think they're way off base."

"Did you tell Detective Ross that?"

"Has he talked to you?" Haley asked.

Shelby seemed surprised by the question. "Isn't he staying at your house?"

"Yes, but we don't exactly have heart-to-hearts, if you know what I mean."

Shelby's smile made her face radiate warmth. "I know exactly what you mean. My husband and I were once forced to spend hours on end together. That was before we got married and long before I was willing to admit that what I felt for him was a whole lot more than simple chemistry."

"Dalton and I do not have chemistry," Haley stated. She hated the fact that it sounded more like a whine than a statement born of honest conviction. Shelby and Barbara smiled at each other. It was one of those exchanges that confirmed all of Haley's secret suspicions. Her friends were obviously reading more into her reactions to Dalton. "Can we get back to the issue of Claire?"

Shelby took one of the unoccupied chairs, sat down and folded her hands in front of her.

Joleen, the newest addition to the Rose Tattoo staff, appeared in an instant. The woman's face was marred by deep lines and a sort of vacancy behind her washed-out brown eyes. Shelby's presence seemed to make her somewhat nervous, but the forced smile seemed to come naturally, as if she'd spent a lifetime putting up a brave front.

"I'd like some iced tea," Shelby said. "How about you all?"

"I'm full," Haley answered.

Joleen cleared Haley's plate and hurried off toward the kitchen.

"If Rose finds out you're eating like a bird, she might just come out here and force-feed you," Shelby said.

"Then don't tell her. She's been sending Susan over every day with enough food to feed an army. If it wasn't for Malcolm and his Merry Men, I'd have to invest in a second refrigerator to handle the excess."

"Detective Ross is a big man. I would think he would require a lot of calories."

"I thought I could count on you, Shelby. Please don't jump on this bandwagon. I'm not interested in

Detective Ross and I wish everyone would just accept that.''

"Then you won't want to know that he came in about an hour ago," Shelby said. "He's been upstairs with Rose."

"Doing what?"

"He's been talking to us about Claire."

"At least he's finally doing something," Haley grumbled. "I was beginning to think that he was going to grow roots on my sofa with that damned cell phone stuck to his ear."

"He's really convinced that Claire was somehow involved with the stabbing," Shelby explained. "He kept asking us about Claire's personal habits. He seemed to want to know if she was involved with drugs."

Haley was on her feet before the last syllable fell from Shelby's mouth. Urged on by a sudden burst of anger, she smacked open the kitchen door and stomped past the shocked faces of the staff. As she climbed the stairs, she began to plan her statement. There was no way she was going to let him get away with this. No way she would allow him to sully Claire's name and reputation just to bolster his own ridiculous theory that she had somehow decided to commit attempted murder.

Haley knocked once, then pushed open the office door without waiting for a response. Neither of the occupants even flinched. In fact, Rose's mouth twitched as if she might be battling a grin.

Dalton was seated in one of the chairs, his denim-clad legs crossed casually at the ankles. Haley glared at him as she mumbled a hostile greeting to Rose.

"What are you trying to do by insinuating that Claire abuses drugs?"

"Investigate," he replied.

The fact that he didn't bother to react to her tone or the volume of her voice only served to further incite Haley's anger. "You haven't been investigating. You've been parked at my house like it was some sort of spa for lazy police detectives. You've done nothing but talk on the phone and eat for the past week."

At least that got a rise out of him, albeit a small one. His eyes burned amber like the flames of a flash fire. Then his face became a mosaic of hard angles and tense muscle.

"Haley, don't you think you're overreacting just a little? The man is only doing his job."

"Rose," Haley began, though her fierce eyes never left Dalton's face, "he isn't doing his job. Assassinating Claire's character and ruining her reputation is hardly a real investigation."

"I'm following up on a lead we got this afternoon."

It didn't sound like an apology or even a defense.

Dalton's statement was just that, nothing more. Flat, unemotional and detached.

"Your lead is way off base. The only substances Claire ever abused were hair-care products."

Rose snickered, then stood and made some excuse to leave the room.

"Don't give me that, Haley. You should have been up-front with me from the beginning. It would have saved us both some time."

"What are you talking about?"

"Don't pretend, Haley. Protecting Claire is admirable, but it hasn't done anything but send me in circles and waste my time."

Fuming, Haley clenched and unclenched her hands as she took a step closer to him. For once, the scent of his cologne did little more than elicit the briefest distraction. Good, she told herself. Finally her intellect was back in control of her body.

"Instead of slandering Claire, you should be concerning yourself with the blood you found in her house. Or maybe you *should* find Justin or the ex-boyfriend. Or, if it isn't too taxing, maybe you could follow up on the fax journal Barbara found in Claire's office."

Dalton slowly rose to his full height. She hated the fact that she had to tilt her head back in order to maintain eye contact. She also hated the fact she felt the tiniest bit of apprehension when she noted the blatant hostility emanating from him.

"Don't presume to tell me how to do my job, Counselor."

The last word came out sounding very much as if it had left a foul taste in his mouth.

"Is that what this is about?" she demanded as she stood toe to toe with the large man. "Does your irrational dislike for my profession make it okay for you to slander my friend? Is she now guilty by association?"

"At least you are capable of telling the truth."

"What?"

"You were right on when you implied that I'm not real keen on attorneys. I bust my butt to make a case and you guys make sure the defendant has more rights than the victims."

"Spare me the philosophical—and might I add incorrect—condemnation of my profession and try to stick to the topic. Why haven't you done your job?"

"I've been busy baby-sitting you," he thundered back.

"Not at my request," she returned in the same tone. "I've told you since day one that I didn't want you in my house."

"And I've told you that until we have Claire in custody, you're a potential victim and I'm supposed to prevent crime."

"Then start by trying to be objective. Do a real investigation instead of trying to come up with some lame rationalization to support your flawed theory that Claire had anything to do with the attack."

Dalton reached into the breast pocket of his jacket and pulled out several sheets of neatly folded paper. He shoved them against her chest.

"The results of my investigation, Ms. Jenkins."

Snatching the pages, Haley unfolded them and began to read. She was vaguely aware of the sound of his short breaths as she read the pages a second time. A lot of the anger seemed to drain from her, leaving her feeling stunned and deflated.

"This can't be right," she said as she held the papers out to him. "It has to be another Claire Benedict. Or some sort of snafu with the computer system at the police department."

He shook his head, then ran one hand through his hair to push it off his deeply tanned forehead. "You won't give up, will you?"

"I know Claire Benedict and I know she was never arrested for drug possession."

"God, you *are* a lawyer. You have a rationalization for everything. Even when it's right there in front of you in black and white."

"And you don't listen. I know Claire. She does not do drugs."

"Then she could have been buying it for her boyfriend. Or Justin."

Dalton had never taken the report from her, so Haley took her finger and tapped at the top line on the first page. "This report is dated two months ago. Justin was still in jail and she hadn't yet started seeing the boyfriend. Besides, if Claire had gotten into trouble, she would have asked me to defend her."

"Maybe she didn't want her friend, the paragon of virtue, to know that she had this kind of problem."

"Maybe you just can't accept that I'm not like you and your cronies."

"What does that mean?"

"Are you going to try and tell me that cops aren't notorious for abusing alcohol? Then your brotherhood protects and conceals them from the innocent, unsuspecting public."

"If you're planning on an entrapment defense by attacking my department, good luck."

Couldn't anything get through to him? "Dalton?" she asked as she reached out and placed a tentative hand on his arm. "Please listen to me. I know you believe the worst of Claire but I'm telling you, she wasn't an addict and she would never want to hurt me. You have to try to find Justin or that other loser. You have to find out what was in the faxes she received that might have caused her to go into hiding. You have to find out why she didn't keep her appointment with Dr. Dixon and why there was blood at her house. Please?"

Dalton looked up at the ceiling before he gently wrapped his square-tipped fingers around her upper arms. The anger was no longer burning in his eyes.

In fact, he looked almost remorseful as he took two long breaths.

"I've done most of those things already, Haley."

"What?"

"I had the lab type the blood we found in Claire's foyer."

"And?"

"I had Dr. Tate's office send over her medical records. The blood type didn't match. Someone might have been injured at that house but it wasn't your friend Claire."

Chapter Seven

"Are you going to tell me his name?"

Dalton eased his car into the narrow opening of the garage under the building that housed her office. Haley had been unusually quiet since their heated discussion the previous evening. Her attitude hadn't improved during the ride, either.

"I don't think that would be wise."

"Just like you didn't think it would be wise for me to drive myself to my own office?" she fairly snarled.

He brought the car to a halt in a No Parking zone at the elevators. Twisting slightly, he turned to find her looking at him with angry eyes. "I'm trying to protect you."

The anger didn't fade as she answered, "I don't need protection. You're absolutely wrong about Claire. Since you don't seem willing to investigate—"

"I've *been* investigating," he thundered. "Every

angle leads right back to your friend. That isn't my fault."

"Since you've already convicted her, then you shouldn't care if I know her ex-boyfriend's name."

But I do. I don't know how far you'll go to try and prove Claire Benedict isn't a criminal. "This is a police matter."

Frustration marred her pretty face and he felt himself beginning to bend. "Giving you the guy's name won't do anything but it will compromise my investigation."

She made a small noise and began collecting her briefcase and purse. As she started to open the car door, Dalton reached out and touched the sleeve of her crisp suit. She stilled, but she didn't look at him.

"I have to go," she said. "I've got a major meeting this afternoon and I have to prepare."

"I'm not as closed-minded as you think."

"Whatever."

Dalton sighed. "Call the number I gave you when you want to leave the building."

"Whatever."

His fingers tightened for emphasis. "I'm serious, Haley. You aren't to leave your office without protection."

Her only response was to slam the door with enough force to rattle the windows. His eyes followed her as she marched to the elevator and pressed the button. Her hair tumbled well past her squared shoulders. He found himself hoping that she would turn around. Give him some small crumb so he could stop feeling like the heavy. There was no crumb. She stepped inside the elevator without so much as a backward glance.

"What the hell is going on here?" Haley screamed as soon as her brain processed the scene before her.

"Mr. Phelps said you were to go to his office directly," her secretary answered.

"Don't worry." Haley tossed her purse and her briefcase in one of the waiting room chairs and went directly to the office at the end of the hall. Without knocking, she stormed into the room and found Phelps behind his huge mahogany desk. "Am I fired?"

Phelps at least had the decency to look uncomfortable as he swung his arm and invited her to take a seat. "I know this must seem like a shock to you," he said.

Haley stubbornly stood her ground. "Have I been fired?"

"We're in a very delicate situation here—"

"Don't tap-dance," she interrupted. "If you have decided to fire me, I'd like to know."

"It's just temporary at this juncture," Phelps said. "This firm has a long history here in Charleston. Our clients expect privacy and your present…circumstance jeopardizes that."

"Circumstance?" Haley snorted. "I was the victim of a crime. How does that jeopardize the firm?"

"Please sit down," he urged. "If it makes any difference, I was opposed to this action."

Relenting, Haley took a seat and folded her hands in her lap. She didn't know whether to cry or scream. Since neither option was likely to do her any good, she drew her lips into a tight line and waited for whatever pathetic excuse he was going to offer.

"Thank you," Phelps said. He seemed to age before her eyes as he took a fortifying breath. "I know this is disappointing, but the partners feel it would be best for everyone if you took an extended leave of absence."

"Not best for me," Haley returned calmly. "I have several cases nearing trial and the Mulhulland divorce is to the deposition stage. I don't see how tossing me—"

"All of your pending cases have been reassigned to other associates. Of course things will return to normal once this matter has resolved itself."

"What *matter* are we talking about?"

"It is common knowledge that the police believe that Miss Benedict was behind that terrible incident in the park. We'll continue to handle her affairs until these allegations are proved or disproved."

"How kind of you."

Phelps grimaced at her sarcasm.

"You have to look at things from our vantage

point, Haley. Your stabbing has caused the police to become quite interested in this firm's clients. We can't risk the loss of income or any damage to our reputation. I imagine it can't be long before the police release the information that this firm represented Ms. Benedict on drug charges. Many of our more conservative clients will probably—''

"I don't know who told you that," Haley cut in. "Claire was never arrested. She doesn't do drugs and I never represented her."

Phelps seemed surprised by her vehement declaration. "I know that."

Haley relaxed. "Good. Detective Ross is using that misinformation as an excuse to stall a real investigation. It might help if you called him and told him that Claire was never involved with narcotics."

Phelps eyebrows drew together. "You misunderstand me, Haley. I know you didn't represent Miss Benedict in that matter. Mr. Betterman did."

"BETTERMAN?" she grumbled as she turned on the power to her computer terminal. "Before I give you my parting memo, I'll check for myself."

Going into the database, Haley requested Claire's billing records. The small hourglass hung on the screen for a few seconds before the file appeared against the bright blue background. Unfortunately, the billing records confirmed what she'd been told by both Phelps and Dalton. Shaking her head, she tried to come up with some reasonable explanation for what she was seeing. "Why would Claire suddenly start buying cocaine when she was about to conceive a child?"

Taking a pencil from her almost barren desk, she jotted down the date of Claire's consultation with Betterman regarding her arrest. She reached for the phone and dialed Barbara's number.

"Can you get away?"

"Now?" Barbara asked. "Isn't this your grand return to the legal stage?"

"It's turned into a limited engagement," she answered. "Can you get away?"

"What happened?"

"I'll tell you when I see you."

"You're scaring me. Have you heard from Claire?"

"No. Can we please do this in person?"

"Sure. I've got a meeting...."

"That works out great because I have to type a memo and grab a cab."

"A cab?"

"I don't have my car. I'll be at your office in an hour or so."

"I'll be here."

Haley typed the memo and left it in the center of her desk. All of her personal items were in a small box by the door. She was about to leave when she remembered Dalton's edict. It took her a minute to dig his business card out of her purse. The telephone number was written in a bold, masculine hand that suited its owner. She stood holding the card, silently debating the pros and cons of calling him. After a short debate, she slipped the card into her purse and left her office with her box tucked neatly under her arm.

After paying the cabdriver, Haley juggled her briefcase, her purse and the box as she opened the door to Barbara's office.

"You look like a homeless person," Barbara said in greeting. "A beautifully accessorized homeless person, of course."

Haley smiled for the first time in hours. "Can you get away?"

"Sure. We can put your stuff in my trunk while you explain to me why you are traipsing around Charleston with a desk set and your diplomas under your arm."

Haley and Barbara agreed on going to a small coffee shop in the heart of the tourist section before they headed out of Barbara's office.

Haley left her jacket in the car and wished her cream-colored blouse was cotton instead of silk. Heat wafted up from the street in watery waves as the morning sun burned down from a hazy sky.

"You keep looking behind you," Barbara remarked as they walked along the uneven sidewalk.

"I guess it will take some time before I get over what happened in the park."

"I can't believe they put you out to pasture. What kind of jerks do you work for?"

"Heartless ones." Haley sighed as they reached the small restaurant. "I guess I should be happy that it's a paid leave. Malcolm will be thrilled."

A pleasant-looking woman seated them at a table by the front window. The small dining room smelled of freshly baked pastries and chicory-rich coffee.

"Why don't you go out to the beach house?" Barbara suggested. "You can play at the beach and get away from all the noise of that incompetent construction crew."

"Malcolm and his men are slow, but they're very good. The house is beginning to take shape."

"Haley, are we really here to chat about your crazy contractor?"

"Not really, but it beats dwelling on the fact that my hopes for a partnership are down the drain."

"I can't believe they're doing this to you. If they were so concerned about scandal, how come they didn't shut down two years ago when Betterman's wife divorced him after telling the whole world that he couldn't keep his fly zipped?"

Haley smiled again. "I knew calling you was a good idea. You have always been able to make me laugh."

"And I always know when you're stalling. What

gives, Haley? There's something besides the job, right?''

Meeting her friend's questioning eyes, she nodded. "I need to ask you something."

"Do you need money?" Barbara guessed, reaching for her wallet as she asked.

"It isn't money, but thanks." She reached across the table and gave her friend's hand a tight squeeze. "I was wondering if you noticed anything strange about Claire's behavior."

"All of Claire's behavior is strange. That's why we love her."

"I'm serious. Think back over the past couple of months. Did she do or say anything that was really weird?"

"By really weird, do you mean like Susan-weird, or like regular-weird?"

"Regular."

"Other than the baby stuff?"

"Anything at all."

The waitress delivered their coffee while Barbara sat in silent contemplation. Haley knew that Barbara would put two drops of cream in her coffee and three packets of sugar. Haley knew that she would stir the coffee for a long time, then let it sit until it cooled.

"Forget that question," Haley said suddenly as her mind went into overdrive. "Tell me my most annoying habit."

"I think the heat has fried your brain. Where did that come from?"

"Just tell me."

"Okay, I've always hated the way you hang your clothes."

"You have?" Haley asked, surprised.

"C'mon, your closet looks like an expensive kid's shop. Everything is hung as an outfit, no spontaneity. Now, what does my opinion about your closet have to do with your job or Claire's behavior?"

"It simply reinforced my gut feeling that something is wrong here."

"You've suffered a professional mortal injury. I'd say that qualifies as a wrong."

"It has to do with *why* this happened."

"It happened because your law firm is run by a bunch of hypocrites."

"Dalton showed me a copy of a police report from early June."

"Did he? You're losing me, Haley."

"The report said that Claire had been arrested for drug possession."

Barbara laughed. "Has the DEA declared self-centeredness a drug now?"

"I'm serious," Haley told her.

"There has to be some sort of mix-up. Claire would never do drugs. Especially not since she got on this baby kick."

"I agree. Phelps said the real reason I was being

banished was because they didn't want word to get out that the firm was representing Claire on a drug charge.''

"Did you invite me here to tell me that Claire was on drugs? At least that would explain her choice in men. Wait! Maybe Claire is off at some fancy drug rehab. She must have known that Dr. Dixon wouldn't impregnate her if she was on drugs.''

Haley shook her head. "Maybe that's what we're supposed to think.''

Barbara frowned. "What are you saying?''

"You, Claire, Susan and I have been friends forever. We know each other's habits and we spend a lot of time together. You just proved that when you made that nasty remark about my closet.''

"It wasn't nasty and you asked.''

"The point is—" Haley lowered her voice "—I don't think Claire was on drugs.''

"You're starting to sound like an Oliver Stone movie. Why would the police and your law firm conspire to make it look like Claire was on drugs?''

"I don't know.''

"Have you asked Dalton?''

Haley snorted. "Dalton and I don't talk unless we have to.''

"But he's so charming.''

"Charming?'' Haley parroted. "He barely speaks. He couldn't pry his mind open with a crowbar and I don't like him hovering all over me.''

Barbara laughed. "Every other woman in Charleston would probably kill to have a man like that hovering. Are you sure it isn't you?"

"Meaning?"

"If you've been giving him the frosty treatment, it's no wonder he doesn't talk to you. I've seen you brush men off, and it isn't pretty."

"Try the other way around," Haley admitted.

"Come again?"

"He's made it perfectly clear from day one that he isn't interested in me and I think that even if he was, he'd control himself because he has a prejudice against lawyers."

Barbara was gaping. "So turn on the charm."

"I'm not that stupid," Haley countered. "Dalton Ross isn't what I want, so why play with fire?"

Barbara's green eyes glistened with devilish humor. "Because it's fun."

"I have other plans for Detective Ross."

"Such as?"

"He said the blood he found at Claire's house wasn't hers."

"Whose was it?"

"I don't know," Haley said. "But Dalton said that he got Claire's blood type from her records at Dr. Tate's office."

"Dr. Tate won't give them to you, will he?"

"I don't want copies of her records, I just want to look at them."

"Why?"

"Because I remember Claire saying that Dr. Dixon had ordered some blood tests to be done before she saw him. If Dr. Tate did the tests, they probably did a tox screen. If Claire was on drugs, her health records would indicate that."

"And just how do you propose to convince Dr. Tate to let you read confidential medical records?"

"Dalton might have a copy."

"Will he let you see them?"

Haley shook her head vigorously. "He sees me as some sort of major security threat as well as the most unappealing woman on the face of the earth. He won't even tell me the name of that animal who beat Claire to a pulp."

"They found him?"

"He's not where he's supposed to be. I think Dalton has an address, but he isn't going to tell me."

"If he won't tell you and Dr. Tate is forbidden by law from disclosing Claire's records, what do you plan to do?"

"I'm going to wait until Dalton is asleep and see if he has the report."

"That doesn't exactly sound like a foolproof plan."

Taking in a big gulp of air, Haley said, "If I can't get the information from Dalton, I'll have to resort to getting it from Dr. Tate."

"How do you plan on doing that?"

"Claire is missing and I'm terrified something is happening to her. I heard her voice. Something isn't right."

"And you think Dr. Tate will bend the law because of your concerns?"

"No. I'll be the one bending the law. If there's no other option, I'll break into his office."

"Now I know you've lost it," Barbara said. "And I think you'd better stop planning your crime because the cavalry has arrived."

Haley followed Barbara's gaze and her breath stuck in her chest when she saw a very angry Dalton closing in on her. "Ooops."

"Why does he look so furious?" Barbara whispered.

"I'm not allowed to go anywhere without his permission."

"Judging from his expression, you're going to be punished."

DALTON was in the living room with his cell phone glued to his ear. Haley was trying her best to act repentant. Not that she really cared if he was annoyed or not, she just wanted him to go to sleep so that she could get on with her search.

The words of her well-bred mother haunted her as she tossed a second batch of biscuit dough into the disposal. Her mother had always told her that she wouldn't need law school if she could just learn to make good biscuits. It was lucky for her that Dalton had received the obviously private, apparently urgent telephone call.

Haley tried once more to follow her great-grand-mother's recipe. Once again, the runny, unrollable batter was poured down the drain. Disgusted, she yanked open the refrigerator and grabbed a can of ready-made rolls and placed them on a baking sheet. He would just have to live with store-bought rolls to go with the fried chicken and mashed potatoes.

"You look like hell," Dalton said as he joined her in the kitchen.

The retort that sprang to her lips was swallowed as she turned to meet his stony glare. It was unsettling to see that her hours of toiling in the kitchen hadn't mellowed him in the least. In fact, judging from the stern set of his jaw and the fire blazing from his eyes, he was growing angrier, not the reverse.

"Cooking was never my strong suit," she said as she nervously brushed some of the flour from her linen skirt. "I hope you like fried chicken."

"All that fat is bad for you."

Haley looked at his trim, fit body and wanted to kick herself. He was obviously one of those health nuts who only ate fruits, vegetables and that stuff that looked like library paste but tasted worse.

"I made a salad, too," she said as she used tongs to remove the chicken from the frying pan. "You don't have to eat this. Malcolm will—"

"I love fried chicken."

For some reason that little admission made her pulse increase. *Get a grip! Stop acting like you're cooking a cozy dinner for two.* "Good," she managed to squeak out in a small voice.

After telling her the food was good, Dalton ate his meal in silence. Haley felt her nerves being stretched to their limits. All she could do was sneak glances at the wall clock, silently calculating when she might get the chance to look for Claire's medical records.

Dalton never left the kitchen as she cleaned the mess, then announced she was going to bed. Unlike other evenings, he didn't say good-night, he simply nodded his head.

Haley paced in her room for what felt like hours. She so tightly coiled with anticipation that when the grandfather clock chimed the first hour after midnight, she actually shivered.

Slipping her shoes off, she moved down the dark hall with one hand grazing the wall. She stopped at the landing and listened above the frantic beat of her heart. Nothing. Sucking in a breath, she went downstairs and decided it was best to begin by seeing if he had left his jacket in its usual place on the back of one of the kitchen chairs.

She found his jacket. He was wearing it.

"Can't sleep?"

"I...uh...I...no."

His face was illuminated by the moonlight streaming in through the French doors. His expression wasn't quite as harsh as before, but he still seemed distant and aloof.

"I found a bottle of brandy in the cupboard. I hope you don't mind."

"No."

"Want some?"

"Yes."

Haley swallowed, trying to gain some composure as she watched him move around in the shadows. He looked so at home in her kitchen, as if it was the natural place for him to be. *Who are you kidding?* her brain taunted. *He looks good, period.* Too bad they were at cross-purposes. "Thanks," she said as she took the glass from him. There was something about the way he seemed to be watching her that made her uncomfortable.

Haley knew she was attractive. She was used to all sorts of looks. She knew when a man was leering at her or a woman was sizing her up for a catty remark. But she couldn't decode the way Dalton looked at her—and his gaze never seemed to falter.

"Why do you do that?"

"Do what?"

"Stare at me all the time."

Haley wished the room was lighter, then she might be able to see his reaction to her blunt observation.

"I guess I'm not sure what to say."

"Very funny," she commented as she took a fortifying swallow of the brandy and let it burn down her throat. She moved to the door, deciding it was easier to talk to him when she wasn't distracted by those incredible eyes of his. "You don't impress me as the kind of man who goes mute in the company of women."

"I've recently turned over a new leaf."

Haley placed her drink on the counter and lifted the curtain to look out at the moonlight. "What kind of new leaf?"

"The midlife crisis one. I decided that if I wanted to find a wife and start a family, I needed to clean up my act."

"You want that?"

"Sure. I'll be forty soon. I think it's time I grew up."

"It isn't any of my business, but do you really think pretending you're something you aren't is the best way to find a spouse?"

"You're an expert on the subject?"

The teasing tone lightened her spirits. "No. But I was never big on games."

"You think behaving like a proper Southern gentleman is a game?"

"No. But it strikes me that what you're doing is a little bit like what a woman does when a man takes her to dinner and she only eats a salad. Like there's some law that says a man won't marry a woman with a normal appetite."

His laughter caressed her ears. "I see what you mean. So, you think I should just go back to acting like myself and let the consequences be damned?"

"I think that's a better plan than acting like an imitation of Ashley Wilkes. Remember, the women all went for Rhett anyway. Along with two X chromosomes we all get this perverse desire for men who are dogs. Women are famous for thinking they can love a man into the perfect mate."

"Is that what you think?" Dalton asked.

His words were spoken almost against her ear. The mere brush of his chest against her back was her only warning that he had come up behind her. The warning hadn't come quickly enough for Haley to mount a proper defense. She was trapped between his warm body and the cool glass of the door. Before she could twist away, he locked her against him, his arms circling her trembling body. She stood in silence while her mind warred with her body's desire.

"We were talking in generalities."

"What if I was being specific? What if I told you I'd been spending the last week fighting to keep my hands off you?"

It was sheer pleasure when he moved even closer, allowing their bodies to touch from shoulder to thigh. His left hand slid lower, until his fingers splayed over her abdomen.

"I suppose I would have to admit that I've had the same thought."

"You should have said something sooner," he whispered against her ear.

Haley swallowed the moan that seemed to spring from the heat where he was touching her. She could feel his palm through the thin fabric of her skirt, feel the erotic little tingle it inspired. His other hand tugged her blouse free, then he began a slow, sweet push upward from her navel to her rib cage.

After several teasing minutes filled with tentative strokes of his thumb against her flesh, Dalton finally reached up to cup the fullness of her breast. Haley was helpless to stop the moan, helpless to do anything but enjoy the sensations. Dalton nuzzled her neck as he slipped his hand beneath her bra.

His mouth wandered over her neck, leaving a trail of what couldn't really be described as kisses. It was more like he was taking a sampling. His tongue flicked against the side of her throat while his hand on her abdomen began making slow, sensuous circles. When Haley gasped, Dalton laughed softly. It was a sound of pure masculine amusement and delight.

"I've been dreaming of doing this every night we've slept under the same roof," he murmured. "I really want you."

"Dalton, no..." It was a weak protest and he didn't react. She couldn't really blame him. Even to her own ears it sounded like one of those no's that actually mean yes. "Really, Dalton. I don't want this to happen."

His hands stilled and Haley was glad he couldn't see her face. She felt certain the indecision she felt would be evident in her eyes. If he even guessed she was this aroused, there was no way she could put a stop to this lunacy.

"Haley?" Her name came out as a plea.

"I said stop and I mean it."

"Your body didn't say no."

"My body is controlled by my brain, and my brain doesn't want to make this mistake."

Reluctantly, his hands slid off her and he moved away. Haley was left feeling oddly cold and abandoned. *This is what I want,* she reminded herself. *What I want is Dalton, but not like this.*

"Are you sure it isn't that you have something more important to do right now?"

"What?" she asked through the fog of her draining passion.

"You didn't come down here for brandy and kisses. You came down here to see if you could get your hands on Claire's medical records."

Chapter Eight

"Barbara called me," he said as he stepped away from her, turning her to face him in the process. "Your friend thinks that you're about to commit a felony."

She hugged her arms tightly to her body as she looked up at him through her lashes. Looking at her standing there in the moonlight with her lips parted and her breaths coming in short spurts, Dalton found it impossible to be angry with her. The memory of her body molded to his and the knowledge of how warm and soft her skin was made any rational thought a near impossibility.

"I'm simply trying to understand why in the course of ten days my friend has disappeared, I've been stabbed and my career has been flushed down the toilet."

"Then you should have asked me for help."

"I did," she said softly. "I asked for the name of Claire's ex-boyfriend. I've asked—"

"The wrong questions," he finished. "You should have asked me for help."

Her lashes fluttered against her cheeks. "What would I have to do for this help?"

He supposed he deserved that. "Nothing."

"Then why did you...?"

Dalton rubbed his face. "For the usual reason. I do want you, Haley."

"Is that the price for your help?"

"I gave you one free shot," he warned. "Why don't you tell me your conspiracy theory?"

She turned on the light and retrieved her brandy before sitting at the table. Her blouse was disheveled and it served as a reminder of what might have been. What still was if the uncomfortable tightness in his groin were any indication. If he had half a brain, he'd get himself reassigned.

"It isn't a conspiracy really," she began. "Just a whole lot of suspicion about this drug thing."

"I spoke to the arresting officer this afternoon. He's a sergeant who has no history with Internal Affairs and no connection to Claire Benedict. He was a little vague on the details of the bust, but his division averages a couple of hundred-drug possession arrests a month, so that isn't unusual."

"I'll accept that she was arrested. There's no reason Phelps would lie about the firm representing her in the matter. Claire's different trusts and foundations make us a small fortune, so he wouldn't fabricate something like that and risk losing her business.''

Dalton frowned as he looked at her. He gripped the table edge and tried to speak as gently as possible. "Have you prepared yourself for the possibility that Claire might be—''

"Yes, so don't say it. Have you looked into the possibility that someone might have kidnapped her for ransom?''

"There would have been a demand by now.''

Haley slumped in the chair, her hands so tightly wrapped around the glass that her knuckles showed white. That little glimpse of her vulnerability prodded him to go to her and begin to massage the tension at her neck. As he stood inhaling the scent of her hair, he knew it wasn't just the vulnerability. He simply wanted an excuse to touch her—to be near to her. "Barbara said something about blood work?''

"Claire was supposed to have some tests done and have the results sent to Dr. Dixon's clinic.''

"I thought she never saw Dixon,'' Dalton said.

"She didn't. His office gave her a whole list of things to do before the initial consultation. She had a questionnaire, the blood work and a credit check.''

"Credit check?''

"He charges five thousand for artificial insemination. It can run as high as fifty if she needed GIFT or IVF.''

"What is that?''

"GIFT is using donor eggs. IVF is in vitro—test tube baby is the popular term."

"Why didn't she just go out and do it the old-fashioned way?"

"Dr. Dixon specializes in genius sperm and the best and brightest donor eggs. Claire isn't the type to go for anything but the top of the line." Haley reached up and placed her hand on the back of his. "Will you help me?"

"Only if we agree that I'm the one in charge."

"Is that the only condition?"

"Well, I wouldn't say no if you'd offer to let me finish what I started."

"I CAN'T BELIEVE you let her talk you into this," Shelby chided as she bounced a rather unhappy Cassidy on her hip. "Talk some sense into him," she said to her husband.

Dylan Tanner was at the bar, allowing his young son, Chad, to slide along the polished surface in his socks. Rose was upstairs, but that wouldn't have made a difference. Haley knew full well that Chad Tanner was allowed to do anything. His parents were well-known for the unconditional way they loved their son and daughter. It was equally well-known that the children were beautifully behaved despite a total lack of parental discipline.

"I couldn't keep you from interfering with an investigation, remember?'' Dylan called to his wife. ''My sympathies, Detective Ross.''

Haley took Cassidy from Shelby and bounced the eighteen-month-old on her knee. The little girl smelled of powder and her fussiness quickly turned to giggles as Haley went faster and faster.

''You could get hurt,'' Shelby argued. ''You don't know what you're getting into.''

''I've already been hurt,'' Haley said. ''It took me most of the night to get him to agree to this. Don't make me go back to begging.''

Haley met Dalton's eyes. It was like looking at a completely different person. He no longer seemed to stare right through her and she guessed it had something to do with their brief but combustible encounter. The mere thought of the way it felt to be touched by his strong hand brought a tightness to the pit of her belly. She had to keep reminding herself that Dalton was the wrong man.

''So what are you going to do first?'' Susan asked as she emerged from the kitchen, balancing a tray of salt and pepper shakers.

Haley surrendered Cassidy to Shelby as the Tanners began the ritual of saying their goodbyes to the children. She was beginning to understand Claire's sudden desire for a child as she watched the two adults smother the children with kisses and hugs, which were enthusiastically returned. The Tanners were an ideal family, the kind that belonged on a poster.

"Haley?" Susan prompted.

"It seems to me that the best place to start is by retracing all of Claire's movements since she dumped her boyfriend."

"That was almost two months ago," Susan argued. "I saw my psychic last night and she said Claire's aura is faded."

"Aura?" Dalton asked Haley.

She tried not to smile as she shrugged her shoulders and wordlessly warned him not to probe.

Susan, obviously oblivious to everyone's amusement continued. "Madame Kerri said Claire was definitely alive, but her weak aura isn't a good sign."

Haley struggled to stay focused as Susan babbled. Part of the problem was that Dalton had taken the seat next to her and his shoulder brushed her arm. Since she no longer had to work, she was dressed in a sleeveless cotton blouse and pleated shorts. Her hair was piled on top of her head. Everything had been done in an effort to ward off the oppressive summer heat.

Dalton wasn't as lucky. His khaki slacks and oxford shirt had to be some sort of departmental uniform. His hair was still slightly damp from his shower. The scent of soap clung to him as he watched Susan flit around the empty dining room. Haley watched him silently, studying the slight stubble on his chin and the way his lips were pressed together. She couldn't help but wonder what it might feel like to be kissed by this man. *Stop it!* her brain screamed.

"When we went to the cards—"

"Cards?" Dalton interrupted to ask Susan.

"Tarot cards," Haley supplied.

"Right," Dalton breathed, apparently running low on patience.

Susan placed the last set of condiments on a table and let the tray fall to her side. "You're right to go after the boyfriend. The cards told us that the interference with Claire's aura had to do with a man."

"Should I get an arrest warrant?" Dalton teased under his breath.

"If you find the boyfriend, Madame Kerri would be able to take a reading and tell you what he's done with Claire."

"We'll keep that in mind," Dalton said as he stood, taking Haley's elbow as he did. "We'll swing by his place."

A few minutes later, Dalton asked, "Has she always been that loony?"

"Susan isn't mentally ill."

"'Coulda fooled me," he said as they reached his car.

Haley slid into the passenger's seat and left her door open until Dalton had started the car. Hot air spewed from the vents, adding to the stifling temperature.

"Susan is like a lost puppy."

"Mad dog," he countered with a snicker. "Auras and readings. Is she for real?"

"Unfortunately. She wasn't always like this. Believe it or not, she comes from an old Charleston family."

"They must be thrilled to have her out of their hair. How did she get so screwed up?"

"She isn't that bad," Haley defended. "Susan's parents kept her on a tight leash. When she finally rebelled, she *really* rebelled."

"The auras are some sort of rebellion?"

"The auras are tame compared to the cult she gave all her money to."

"She had bucks?"

"Had being the operative word. The summer after we graduated from college, Susan found some guru who was going to teach her the true meaning of life."

"But this truth had a hefty price tag?"

"You got it. By the time the rest of us figured out that the guy was a con artist of the first magnitude, he was long gone."

"So her family disowned her and she's waiting tables at the Rose Tattoo?"

"Nope. Susan's parents would gladly elevate her

social status. Susan says she's happier being her own person."

"And Barbara? What's her story?"

"Barbara is a very independent woman."

"Does she have a bucket of money too?"

Haley smiled at his profile. "She said you had a problem with our socioeconomic situation."

He shrugged. The action caused the material of his shirt to outline his muscular torso. Again Haley experienced that flicker in the pit of her stomach.

"I will admit that I don't have a whole lot of experience with people in your strata."

"I'm not in any strata," Haley insisted. "I work for a living. At least I used to."

"I'm sorry about your job."

"I'm sorry too. I've been working for years to earn a partnership."

"Why?"

Haley blinked. "Why? Because I'm a good attorney and I deserve it."

"Not that," he corrected as he turned on to the Mark Clark Expressway. "I don't understand why you would put up with all those office politics if you didn't have to."

"Do you know how hard it is to make it as a sole practitioner? I would have ended up doing insurance claims and custody cases."

"What do you do now?"

Haley pursed her lips. "Insurance claims and domestic law. But once I made partner, I was hoping to do other things."

"Like what?"

"It doesn't matter now," Haley insisted. "Why are you giving me the third degree?"

"Habit," he sighed. "Sounds to me like your entire life was wrapped up in this partnership thing. No backup plan, huh?"

"I'll figure something out. Right now I'd just be happy finding out what's happened to Claire."

"We will."

She wished she felt as sure as he sounded. With each passing day, her sense of foreboding was growing stronger. "Where are we going?"

"To the last known address of Greg Walsh."

"Is he the scum that beat Claire?"

"The very one," Dalton answered as he exited the expressway and drove into a shabby trailer park at the edge of an industrial section north of town. "According to Claire's phone records, Greg was burning up the phone lines from right there."

Following where he pointed, Haley took in the dirty and tattered structure, which seemed to be listing to one side. The torn remnants of an awning flapped in the hot breeze. As they stepped from the car, an assortment of scruffy animals danced at their feet.

Dalton took his arm and braced her behind him as

they climbed up a set of steps made of weathered wood and cinder blocks. "Let me do all the talking."

"Not a problem," Haley whispered as the scent of rotting garbage reached her nose. She could hear a baby cry and the blare of several television sets from the nearby trailers. It was a depressing place that made her wonder how Claire had ever hooked up with this Greg person.

Dalton's sharp knock rattled the entire building. It also brought a chorus of barks and howls from the collection of stray animals gathered in the dirt roadway.

"You again," grumbled a middle-aged woman with more rollers in her hair than teeth as she opened the ripped screen door. "Greg ain't here."

"Has he been by?" Dalton asked.

"Nope."

The woman peered around Dalton and met Haley's eyes. Her haggard face seemed to harden. "You some sort of police, too?"

"I'm an attorney," Haley answered.

"What do you want with my Greg?"

"It isn't important," Dalton answered. "Make sure Greg calls me when he shows up. Do you still have the card I gave you?"

"I got it." The woman slammed the door and disappeared into the darkened tunnel.

"Why didn't you go inside?" Haley demanded as

soon as they were off the steps. "What if he's in there hiding?"

"He isn't."

"And you know that because?"

He turned and she found herself standing in his long shadow. "I just do. Now, let's see if any of the neighbors are feeling cooperative."

The first three tries were a wasted effort. Apparently the police were not highly respected in this small community. Haley was ready to give up. It was oppressively hot and the sight of small children with bleak and dirty faces was breaking her heart.

"I know Greg Walsh," said a girl who looked no more than fifteen as she shifted a toddler to her other hip. "He's a creep."

"May we come in?" Dalton asked.

The girl shrugged as she wiped damp, dirty, limp hair off her forehead. Haley followed her inside. The interior was clean but cluttered with toys, clothing and an assortment of haphazardly repaired baby items.

"What's your name?" Dalton asked as she went to a cooler and took out a fruit-flavored drink for the toddler on her hip. Haley hid her surprise when this young girl reached back in and got a bottle with nipple. Placing the toddler in a playpen near a noisy fan, she disappeared for a minute, returning with a newborn in her arms.

"My name is Wanda Tremaine. Greg's momma has lived across the way for about a year."

"And Greg?" Dalton asked, reaching down to tickle the child near the fan.

"He comes and goes," she said. "He ain't been around for the past week or so. Neither has Ray Anne."

"Who is Ray Anne?" Haley asked.

"She's Greg's wife."

Chapter Nine

"I can't believe Claire would get involved with a married man," Haley said as soon as they were safely back in the car.

"I'll run his wife's name. Maybe that will turn up a lead."

"Maybe this *is* the lead," she said excitedly. "What if one of the faxes Claire received on the day she disappeared was confirming that Greg was married? Maybe she confronted him and he did something with her."

Dalton didn't seem to share her excitement. "You're assuming that Greg's wife cared about his extracurricular activities."

"Most wives do care when their husband is fooling around on them. Just ask my boss."

"Which boss?"

"Betterman. His wife made life hell for him when she found out he had an appreciation for younger women."

"You can't really equate the Bettermans and the Walshes of this world," he reminded her gently. "When we find Ray Anne, I'll bet she tells us we're welcome to Greg."

"Cynic."

"Realist."

"Where to now?"

"A visit to Dr. Tate. I want to know more about Claire's blood work."

"If it proves that Claire wasn't on drugs, then will you finally believe that something is *truly* wrong?"

Dalton reached over and his fingers closed around her knee. The innocent touch inspired anything but innocent thoughts. Haley held her breath. She didn't dare look at him, afraid that her eyes would betray her. Instead she focused on his hand. His skin was bronzed, slightly callused and warm. There was restrained strength in him, a kind of subdued power that was incredibly sexy.

"I believe something isn't right, Haley. If I didn't, I wouldn't have let you talk me into all this."

Dalton called his office from his cell phone to get additional information on Ray Anne Walsh before they entered the crowded office of Dr. Tate.

Haley felt completely out of place surrounded by women in varying stages of pregnancy. She only felt worse when the women looked from her, then to Dalton, then jumped to the logical conclusion. The women then gave her congratulatory looks, as if Dalton were her trophy.

She smiled nervously as Dalton walked to the receptionist and said something. She was still smiling when he joined her on a sofa against one wall.

"Something funny?"

"I've just never seen a man being ogled before."

He gave her a dark look.

"When we get around to seeing Dr. Dixon, perhaps he'd let you donate some—"

"Don't say another word," he cautioned.

Haley's grin was still firmly in place when they were called back through the maze of hallways to a door marked Private. Dr. Tate had the usual assortment of diplomas and awards on the wall behind his cluttered desk. The artwork consisted of primitive drawings, most signed and dated in childish scrawls and apparently presented to the doctor who had brought the artists into the world. There wasn't much else in the office, except for the posters of the progression of life from conception to birth.

Haley took the seat next to the one Dalton had chosen. "Do you think Dr. Tate will help us?"

Dalton crossed one leg over the other and relaxed his large frame. "I hope so. He was pretty good about providing the information on her blood type."

"What if—"

Haley didn't get to finish her question since Dr. Tate came hustling into the office. He looked kind, harmless and old, everything she liked in a gynecologist. He shook her hand as Dalton made the introductions, then fell into his chair as if this was his first opportunity to sit this month. Judging from the crowd in his waiting room, the man had a lively practice.

"Has there been any word from Ms. Benedict?"

Haley shook her head. "It's like she just vanished."

"I'm sorry," he said earnestly. "Claire spoke of you often over the years."

"How long has Claire been a patient of yours?" Dalton asked.

"Almost fifteen years," he answered without hesitation. "Of course I've seen a great deal of her the past month or so, since I referred her to Dr. Dixon's Women's Center."

"Just like that?" Dalton asked. "I thought Dixon was in demand. How did Claire get in to see him so fast?"

Dr. Tate shrugged. "He must have had a sudden opening. I warned Claire that it could take months to get in to see him. When I spoke to Michael about the referral, he said as much to me."

"You called Dr. Dixon about Claire?" Haley asked.

He nodded. "I have referred patients to him before. Claire wanted to get started right away, so I called Michael's office to see what I could do on this end to speed the process."

"Did you speak directly to Dr. Dixon?" Dalton asked.

"Yes. I happened to catch him between procedures. We had a brief discussion, then he faxed me a list of things we could do here."

"And there was nothing on the list that seemed unusual to you?" Dalton queried.

Dr. Tate's brows drew together and he sat pensive for a moment. "I was a little surprised by the questionnaire."

"How so?" Haley asked.

"It seemed a bit...lengthy."

"Lengthy?" Dalton prompted.

"I must admit," Dr. Tate said, "I fail to see what the potential mother's hobbies have to do with a fairly simple procedure."

"Do you still have Claire's questionnaire?" Dalton asked.

"I have the fax, but I made a copy and gave it to Claire to fill out and send directly to Dr. Dixon."

"May I see it?" Dalton asked.

The doctor shrugged. "I can't see how that would violate Claire's right to privacy."

He pressed a button on the intercom on his desk, summoning his assistant. He instructed the woman to get Claire's file. "I don't see how this will help you," he said. "It is my understanding that Claire never kept her appointment with Dr. Dixon."

"That's correct," Haley said. "Which must seem as strange to you as it does to me. You know how much this meant to Claire."

The doctor nodded. "Michael called me a couple of days afterward to ask me about Claire."

"Is that usual?" Dalton asked.

"Most women who choose artificial insemination as an alternative method of conception are quite committed to seeing it through."

A nurse came in and dropped a rather thick file on Dr. Tate's desk. Using the colored tabs along the edge, he turned to a specific place in the file near the top and began to remove a sheet of paper from the pile. "I'm sorry I didn't have Claire provide me with a copy of this. It would have been simple to have her fax one to me when she sent it to Michael."

"She had already furnished Dr. Dixon with this questionnaire before the appointment?" Haley asked.

"This, a copy of her chart here and the results of the blood work we did."

"About that blood work," Dalton began. "Did you by chance run a screening for drugs?"

Dr. Tate seemed genuinely surprised by the question. "I did, but only because Michael requires it as part of the patient workup."

"Then you have no knowledge of Claire having a history of substance abuse?" Dalton asked.

"Claire Benedict? I only wish all my patients were as fit as she is. That woman takes impeccable care of herself."

"Are we going to Dr. Dixon's office?" Haley asked as he steered toward North Charleston.

"Nope. We're going to my place."

"What for?"

He stole a quick glance at her and chuckled at her shocked expression. "I know you'd like to keep at this, but I'm not that bunny on TV. I need food."

"Oh."

"I'll make something quick, then we can get right back to work."

"We could have stopped at my house," she said, a twinge of annoyance in her tone.

"And listen to Malcolm and his beer-swigging buddies hammer, drill and saw themselves into a stupor? I'll pass, thanks."

"You should be used to it by now."

"Don't worry, Haley. I'll eat fast. I promise I won't even chew."

"I guess I am being a little pushy, huh?"

"You're always pushy."

"You aren't exactly a laugh a minute, either."

"Yes I am," he teased as he gave her a wink. "You just don't know the real me."

He could sense she was watching him as he drove the rest of the way to his town house. He tried to think back to when he had packed, wondering how much of a disaster the place would be. One thing he had learned during his days with Haley was that the woman was positively anal when it came to neatness. With the exception of the mess from the construction, her whole house was organized, right down to the spices being in alphabetical order in the spice rack.

"I can't make any guarantees," he warned as they reached the front door. "I'm not into housekeeping."

Dalton was somewhat relieved when he tried to look at his house with an objective eye. It wasn't perfect, but it was a hell of a lot better than Wanda's trailer. "The kitchen is in the back. Want something?"

"What's on the menu?"

Tossing his keys on the counter, he opened the refrigerator and began to take inventory. Frowning, he shut the door and turned to face her. Haley was perched on one of the bar stools, her shapely legs peeking out at him. "I'm afraid the transformation is complete."

"What?"

"It seems my leftovers have become science projects. I'll call the seafood place up the street. Is that okay?"

"A shrimp salad would be great. Whole wheat, lettuce, no mayonnaise."

"Boring," Dalton teased as he walked past her to

grab the telephone. Dialing the number from memory, he fixed his eyes on Haley, quietly admiring her as she sat with her back to him. He placed the order while a fantasy began to take shape in his head. He couldn't seem to stop himself. He didn't really want to.

"It will take about thirty minutes," he said. "I've got wine or soda."

"Water."

"Even more boring than shrimp salad without mayo."

"Am I here for lunch or a critique?" she teased back.

Dalton grabbed a bottle of water from the frig and took it to her, holding it just out of her reach. "Admit it, Haley. You lead a very dull life."

Her blue eyes grew wide and sparkled playfully. She had never looked more beautiful.

"How can you say my life is boring when I've been stabbed and practically fired all in one week?"

"This week has been an exception," he countered as he lowered the bottle to her cheek, letting it rest against her flawless skin. "You look hot."

"It's w-warm out," she stammered as her eyelids fluttered down, shielding her eyes.

"I wasn't talking about the sultry Carolina weather," he said as he placed the bottle on the counter and put his hand on her face.

"What are you doing?"

"I'm simply following your advice," he said as he allowed his thumb to trace the contour of her cheekbone. Her skin felt flushed and warm.

"When did I advise you to do this?"

"I think you compared me to that mealy-mouthed Ashley Wilkes character."

"I was illustrating a point," she argued, though she made no move to push his hand away. "I wasn't suggesting that you and I..."

"Well, I am," he said as he slipped his fingers beneath her chin and tilted her face to his. "I don't happen to have a carpeted staircase at my disposal, so I'll just improvise."

Dalton stepped closer to her, insinuating himself between her thighs as he dipped his head and took his first tentative taste of her lower lip. He made sure the kiss was light as his hands reached up into her hair.

As his mouth explored hers, he found the pins holding her hair and pulled them free, allowing them to fall to the floor without a thought. It felt too good to think about anything other than the warmth of her mouth. He was a man with a purpose, driven by some inner demon to make certain this was an invitation she wouldn't want to refuse. He made it more than a kiss. It was a seduction and a deliberate one.

Not wanting to scare her off, he made sure each movement, each little flick of his tongue was calculated to give her only a glimpse of what it would be like between them. His fingers raked through the curly mane of her hair, until he could feel the outline of her spine through her thin blouse. She made a small sound as his fingertips began exploring every curve, every nuance.

When her palms flattened against his stomach, it had the impact of a sucker punch. His breath swelled in his chest and he deepened the kiss. There was nothing overtly sexual in the way her hands molded against him, yet it was the most erotic thing he had ever experienced. His determination to make her want him was backfiring. He wanted her so much at that instant, he wasn't sure he would last through the next few minutes.

"Haley?" he questioned against her mouth. Lifting his head, he looked down into her passion-filled eyes. "If you're going to say no, please say it now."

Her answer was a shy smile as she moistened her lower lip with the tip of her tongue. Dalton realized he was holding his breath.

Then he realized his cell phone was ringing.

"Damn," he breathed as he grabbed the thing off his belt and flipped it open. "Ross," he barked into the receiver.

As he listened, he watched the desire and immediacy draining from her eyes. By the time he was finished with the call, he knew there was no way to recapture the moment, not now. But he would—and *soon.*

"What is it?" she asked as she twisted her hair up into a loose mass. "Dalton?"

"Remember the fax journal?"

"Of course."

"One of the numbers was from Baltimore."

A sudden excitement brightened her face. "You've found one of the people Claire talked to the day she disappeared?"

"We got a telephone number for the location that sent the fax a few days ago. We've been trying to contact the person, but we never got an answer."

"So what do you do now?"

Dalton took her hands in his. "I did something, Haley. I called Baltimore and requested they send a unit over to the address."

"So why do you look like your favorite hunting dog just died?"

Lifting her hands to his mouth, he kissed her knuckles. "Claire's fax came from National Investigative Services."

"Who or what are they?"

"It's a guy that specializes in discreet investigations. According to the Baltimore PD, he walks a fine line. Apparently this guy is well-known for illegal entries, wiretaps, anything he can think of to get what the client wants."

"What was he doing for Claire?"

"We'll never know. He was killed in a fire the night after Claire disappeared. The fire destroyed his office and any records that might have answered that question."

"Was it murder?"

"According to Baltimore, the cause of the fire is undetermined."

"Great."

Chapter Ten

"I've never heard of Stan Jackson or National Investigative Services," Barbara said. "Why would Claire hire a private detective from Maryland when Gabe probably would have done it for free?"

"Maybe she didn't want Rose's son to know what she was worried about," Dalton suggested.

"How did you know Gabe was Rose's son?" Haley asked as she passed him the basket of bread.

"I told him," Rose said as she came to their table and took the fourth chair. "I suggested that he ask Gabe for help. Gabe doesn't have to pay attention to the constitution the way this one does."

"Rose," Haley warned. "That isn't a solution. Besides, I would never ask Gabe to do something illegal."

"No, you'd just do it yourself," Barbara quipped. "Haley was all set to break into offices just to prove that Claire isn't a junkie."

"Where did you get a fool notion like that?" Rose

demanded. "That woman wouldn't put a foreign substance in her body."

Dalton leaned over to Haley and whispered, "I guess that doesn't include some stranger's sperm."

"Behave," Haley said as she gave him a little shove.

"What is this?" Rose asked, her drawn-on eyebrows arched above her green eyes. "The two of you seem to be getting on."

"Stop it, Rose," Haley warned.

"Trust me, Rose, nothing major has happened. Haley doesn't have that *look*."

"Barbara!" Haley squealed as she felt her face flame. "Try and remember that you're supposed to be my friend."

"Don't stop now," Dalton urged. "What look are we talking about?"

Haley was mortified.

"It's been too long, Dalton. I can't remember. I think—"

"I think I'll excuse myself," Haley said as she leapt from the table, knocking her chair backward. She fled toward the ladies' room with the three of them laughing in her ears.

"You're Haley Jenkins, right?"

Haley stopped splashing water on her beet-red face and looked at the speaker's reflection in the mirror. "Yes. You're Jaylinn, right?"

The woman smiled but the action didn't reach her eyes. "Yes."

"I wasn't running out on the check," Haley said. "I just came in here to—"

"I never thought that, miss," she said before slipping one hand into the pocket of her uniform apron and pulling out a folded note. "He asked me to give this to you. Since you were sitting with that nice-looking gentleman, I thought it might be best if I gave it to you when you were alone."

"Thanks," Haley said as she accepted the paper. Jaylinn left as soon as the task was completed, leaving Haley alone in the rest room. Breaking the seal on the envelope, she slipped her finger inside and pulled out the note. *What man would be sending me a note?*

When Haley opened the paper, something fell to the floor. As she bent to pick it up, she stopped in midaction.

"ALL I KNOW is that the picture was taken with decent-quality equipment," the crime-scene technician said as he handed Dalton the photograph in a clear plastic bag. "I'll know more once I get it back to the lab. Are you going to bring it down, or should I?"

Dalton gave the young man a warning look in the dashed hope that it might erase the smirk from his face. "I'll bring it down later. I don't want this...*evidence* passed around the whole damned department.''

"I can understand that," Barbara teased. "I guess it would be a little tough to explain to your boss what you were doing playing kissy-face with Haley."

"You aren't helping," Haley groaned as she leaned against the credenza in the office Rose and Shelby shared on the top floor of the Rose Tattoo.

He wished there was something he could say, but the truth was, the picture said it all. Whoever took it had been outside his town house that afternoon, that much was clear. The guy had managed to catch them at the height of passion. His lieutenant was going to have his butt.

"Maybe you could take it to one of those places and have it made into Christmas cards," Barbara suggested. "That pose certainly does roast your chestnuts."

"Shut up, Barbara," Haley pleaded. "Why don't you run on home and put some of that stuff on your face that is supposed to lessen wrinkles."

"Meow." Barbara chuckled as she stood and left the room. "You two behave."

"I'm sorry," Haley said as soon as they were alone.

"I'm pissed," Dalton answered as he disgustedly tossed the picture on the desk. "My boss will probably pull me off this case when he sees this."

"I hope not," Haley said, genuine disappointment in her tone.

That small phrase gave Dalton hope that he wasn't the only one interested in pursuing whatever was starting between them.

"I don't want another detective trying to find Claire. It would be a waste of time if you had to get someone else up to speed."

So much for hopes. "I've got a guy in processing who owes me a few favors. I'll have him do the workup and see how long I can stall before this becomes common knowledge."

"Will you get into trouble?"

He shrugged. "It won't exactly be a plus in my personnel record. I'll deal with it, don't worry."

"Why would someone take a picture of us?"

"I have a feeling the guy was taking a picture of you."

"You think the same person that stabbed me took this picture?"

"I think someone wants to make absolutely sure that you know you're being watched."

"Why?" she asked, as she began rubbing her arms as if suddenly chilled.

Jaylinn Douglas knocked, then came into the room, her graying head bowed. "Rose said I was supposed to come up."

"Please sit down," Dalton said to the timid waitress. "I need to ask you about the note you delivered to Miss Jenkins."

"I didn't know it was anything bad," Jaylinn insisted. "He seemed like a decent man and he sat there watching you for a little bit."

"He was here?" Haley asked.

Jaylinn nodded. "He sat at the bar. Drinking Dewar's Scotch, I think. You could ask Mark, the bartender. I only spoke to him for a minute, then he gave me the note."

"What did he look like?"

"Kind of average height, but, then, he was sitting down. He had brown hair."

"Eyes?" Dalton asked without looking up from his notepad.

"I didn't notice. Mark might have. Want me to send him up?"

"Please."

Dalton looked up and found Haley deep in thought. Some women would have fallen apart by now, but she seemed to be holding up. His admiration *almost* equaled his desire. But then as the picture proved, his desire was pretty strong. He picked it up off the desk and slipped it into the pocket of his shirt.

Mark arrived a few seconds later. Dalton guessed he was somewhere in his mid-twenties. He wore his blond hair long and walked with the arrogance that only a twenty-something bartender could muster.

"Rose said I had to talk to you," he said, openly ogling Haley. For some reason, that riled Dalton.

"There was a guy at the end of the bar tonight," Dalton began, then finished with the brief description Jaylinn had started. "Can you tell me anything else about him?"

"He's been in before," Mark said. "Maybe a half-dozen times in the past few months."

"Was Ms. Jenkins here when he was?"

Mark shook his head. "I don't think so. Not that I can recall, at least. What did he do?"

"Nothing," Dalton answered. "He's a photographer."

"Cool," Mark responded. "I'm a musician."

You're a loser, Dalton thought. "Thanks. That's all."

"You look shook up, Haley. Want me to ask Rose if I can give you a lift home? I saw Barbara leave a few minutes ago."

"I'll see to *Ms.* Jenkins," Dalton said firmly.

"Cool," Mark said with his arms raised in mock surrender.

As soon as he had left the room, Dalton stood, stuffing his notepad in his pants pocket.

"If you were abrupt with Mark because you think he had something to do with this, you're wrong. He's harmless."

"He's got the hots for you," he said.

"He's a kid," Haley protested.

"Tell that to his libido."

Dalton led her down the back stairs and into the alley between the Rose Tattoo and the dependency building that now housed a small club. Rose had told him that the club was only open on weekend evenings.

"Maybe the stabbing and Claire disappearing aren't connected," Haley suggested as soon as they got into the car. "That photo was about me, not Claire."

"Too coincidental," Dalton told her. "I'm beginning to think everything is connected somehow."

"If that's true, Claire could be in real danger."

If she isn't long dead. "I think we'd better find a safe place for you. I'm sure this guy knows where you live. He knows my address now."

"We could go to the beach," Haley suggested.

"We'd never get a room at this time of year."

"I have a house at the beach," she explained. "I haven't stayed there for years."

"Who knows about the beach house?"

"No one but close friends."

"Including Claire?"

"Of course."

Dalton rubbed his chin. "Maybe just for tonight. Tomorrow I'll see what I can do about relocating you to a secure location."

"Forget that," Haley stated. "I want to be where Claire can contact me."

"You aren't making this easy for me, Haley."

"I have that reputation." She sighed. "But please understand how I feel. If it is at all possible, Claire will contact me."

"What about the others?"

"She'll try me first," Haley insisted.

"THIS IS REALLY BEAUTIFUL," he told her as he came up behind her on the balcony, slipping his arms around her small waist. Moonlight illuminated the waves crashing gently just beyond the dune. "Why are you bothering with that mausoleum downtown when you can live here?"

"Kiawah is great," she murmured as she leaned into him. "I guess I like the convenience of town."

"I like the way you look in that robe," Dalton said against her ear. "I like a lot of things about you."

"Do you like my closet?" Haley asked.

"I don't know what your closet has to do with anything," he said as his tongue flicked her earlobe. "Do you have any idea what you look like in the moonlight with your hair all wild from the breeze?"

"Not really."

"It's so incredible that I think I'd better show you instead of trying to explain." Dalton scooped her into his arms and carried her into the living room. The bedroom was too far, so he decided to improvise. Using one foot, he tossed all the cushions from the furniture into a pile on the floor, then carefully lowered them both down to the cushions.

"I like that," he said as he began to taste her neck.

"I haven't done anything."

"You're touching me."

"Oh."

"Touch me more."

Dalton took one hand and fanned her hair out against the pillow. His other hand was busy trying to unfasten her robe. His mouth wasn't idle. He sought and found the ultrasensitive spot near her collarbone and was rewarded by feeling her shiver beneath him. His hand traveled up to grip her shoulder. With his heartbeat increasing, Dalton told himself it was the fascinating fragrance clinging to each strand of her hair, not the fact that for the first time in his life his mind was as involved as his body.

"You always smell like a woman." His voice cracked slightly, but she didn't seem to notice. That knowledge only added to the tightness in his stomach.

His other hand went to her shoulder and he tugged her closer to him. She felt soft beneath him and he silently decided not to think about the tenderness he felt almost as strongly as the desire rushing through him. Her head fell back against the cushions as her pale eyes met his. Her pupils were dilated. They caught and held the faint light, turning into lush, shimmering pools. The sound of her breathing fanned the fires burning deep in the pit of his gut. His thumb found its way to her chin, then ventured further, to the gentle slope of her lower lip.

His heart was pounding in his ears and Dalton knew it was time to decide. He also knew there could be no other decision. He felt as if he'd waited a lifetime for this moment. Tentatively, his hand fanned out against her cheek, leaving his thumb to rest against her slightly parted lips. Her breath was warm where it spilled over his hand. His eyes fixed on her mouth as his fantasies began to mingle with the reality of being so close to perfection.

"Dalton, I..."

Dalton wondered if she knew how incredibly sexy her voice was. He doubted it.

She moved closer to him, until he could feel the outline of her body molding against him. Restraint, once his watchword, was becoming a foreign concept.

When her tongue flicked out to moisten her lower lip, he followed the movement with the pad of his thumb. His action caused her mouth to open further and her hands moved up and captured fistfuls of his shirt. When she raised herself against him, Dalton swallowed the groan in his throat. The heat in his stomach had moved lower, inspiring a whole new array of fantasies.

"Dalton."

He heard his name at about the same time he felt

her begin to push him away. He desperately wanted to struggle against her hands, continue this sweet exploration for the next several hours.

"Dalton."

"Not again," he pleaded.

"Yes, again," she groaned. "Your damned cell phone is ringing again. We're cursed."

Chapter Eleven

"What was it?" she asked as he fell back on to the cushions.

"Nothing urgent," he promised her. "Just my office checking in. Now, back to the important stuff?"

Haley smiled at him. "What if I've lost interest?"

Slowly, deliberately, he eased his hand around her back, until his fingers entwined in strands of silky hair. She looked at him, her head tilted back and her lips slightly parted.

"I care about you," he said.

She said nothing but he felt her lean in to him. That would have to be enough for now. It was all the encouragement he needed. His mouth met hers, forceful and demanding.

With their mouths joined together, she slipped her hand inside his shirt, caressing him. Her actions quickened his need. He sat up, with Haley draped across his lap.

"Don't go anywhere," he said against her lips as

he moved away from her to shrug out of his shirt. He dropped it on the floor and placed his hands on her shoulders.

For a brief instant he looked into her heavy-lidded, thickly-lashed eyes. Finding no resistance, he pushed. She tumbled backward and he moved with her, covering her small body with his own.

The feel of her beneath him was powerfully erotic. He reached for her wrists and caught them in his hands. Gently, he moved her hands above her head. He tasted her hungrily, anxious to know every part of her.

He was only vaguely aware of her perfume. All his senses seemed to be locked on the slow gyrations of her hips. There it was again. The unexpected passion that aroused him beyond belief. He prayed for control.

Dalton tore away from her mouth and pressed his lips against the pulse point at her throat. All the while, he was attentive to keep her hands safely above her head. A small, guttural sound escaped from her when his mouth traveled lower, kissing her through the silk fabric of her robe. He felt her move then, trying to free her hands.

"In a minute," he promised her as he nuzzled the valley between her firm, rounded breasts.

"Please, Dalton?"

"Not yet," he said as he bent his leg and insinuated himself between her thighs. It was his turn to moan.

With his free hand, he smoothed the few strands of hair away from her face, then made a trail from her brow to her lower lip. Her tongue flicked out to moisten his fingertip, nearly sending him over the edge.

Sliding up, he again found her mouth as his hand began a slow descent, over her collarbone until he felt the slope of her breast in his palm. He felt pressure as she strained against his hand and again tried to free her wrists.

"Dalton," she said urgently against his mouth.

He lifted his head and saw the fire in her eyes. When his hand closed over her breast, Dalton watched, fascinated, as her lips parted on a sudden breath. It was a heady experience watching her reaction as his thumb grazed her erect nipple. It pleased him immeasurably to see her reaction, to feel her response. He didn't think she was ready to admit any genuine feeling for him, but this was enough—for now.

"I want to make love to you," he managed in a hoarse voice.

"Obviously, I want that, too," she answered urgently.

He barely allowed the final syllable before his mouth was again on hers. He teased her with his fingers. Alternating the stroke and the pressure until he began to feel her wriggle beneath him. He let go of her wrists.

Her fingers were all over him. Haley felt such urgency. Her heart was beating in her ears. Her skin felt hot from the exhilaration surging through her veins. Not being able to touch him had only made her more determined. Now unencumbered, she began peeling away the remainder of his clothing. She leaned forward and placed a kiss against the soft hair and muscle.

When her fingers found their way to his belt buckle, Haley smiled when she heard the breath hiss through his clenched teeth. It was his turn to be the recipient of this most exquisite form of torture.

He propped himself on his elbow and looked down at her. He was motionless as he allowed her to caress his hard, muscular arms and shoulders. The hair on his chest was as dark as the ebony, disheveled mass framing his attractive face. Haley's hands moved again and she tugged at his belt.

He responded by teasing her nipple again. A sexy half smile punctuated his expression. He slid from the bed of cushions and held his hand out to her. Haley joined him in the stream of moonlight filtering through the window.

His chest was so broad, and she marveled at the way the hair tapered across his taut stomach in a V before disappearing into his opened waistband. It naturally drew her attention.

"If you keep looking at me like that, I'll probably lose it and tear your clothes off."

"No need," she said as her head tilted back. As he watched, she slowly peeled the sleeves away from her shoulders at a deliberately teasing pace. The robe fell away, revealing the edges of her lacy bra. Dalton needed no more encouragement.

He kicked her robe into the pile with his shirt. His eyes roamed over her exposed skin. He dropped to his knees, his open mouth fell against her stomach. She massaged the corded muscles at his shoulders while he placed warm kisses on the sensitive flesh just above her waist. Haley grabbed his head and groaned.

When he rose to his full height, he took Haley with him. They floated back to the cushions. Dalton placed her against the pillows, then shed what remained of his clothes. She gaped in muted admiration when he was next to her, devouring her with his eyes.

He felt her roll against him as he joined her. He allowed himself the pleasure of watching as he ran his palm over her full breasts and flat stomach. He teased her by dipping his fingertips beneath the waistband of her black lace panties. He loved watching the way her eyelids fluttered each time he explored a new area of her supple body.

As he removed her remaining garments, Dalton kissed the part of her he had uncovered. Her skin was flawlessly soft and pale beneath his hand. He could gladly have spent hours exploring every tantalizing inch of her.

"Please," she breathed.

"Please what?" he countered as he reached to stroke the sensitive skin at the inside of her thigh.

"Please?" she repeated in an urgent whisper.

Dalton covered her, carefully positioning himself so that he could watch her face. She caught her lower lip in her teeth when he entered her. He stopped, long enough for her to get used to him. The slow circular motion of her hips told him all he needed to know. Slipping one hand beneath her waist, he arched her against him but made certain he could still see her expression. He watched her intently as their bodies found a primitive rhythm. He watched her eyes, her mouth, her lips.

He felt her reach for him once, then apparently Haley settled for massaging his chest with urgent fingers. Her eyes closed as she moved in unison with him. When she wrapped her legs around him, he found himself buried blissfully deeper. He felt her muscles begin to tense and, as she clutched him, Dalton experienced wave after wave of fierce satisfaction.

He lay next to her, cradling her in his arms. He could feel each breath against his skin and heard her contented sigh. The sound brought a purely egotistical smile to his lips.

She was curled against him, all legs and warm skin.

"I guess I should tell you about that call," he began.

"What do you mean?" she purred as she traced the outline of his nipple with her fingernail.

"There's something I haven't told you," he said as he brushed her temple with a kiss.

"If you're married, I'll kill you."

He chuckled softly. "Nothing like that."

Haley felt her muscles relax. She had been holding her breath, bracing herself for some more important revelation. She placed her lips against his bared chest and drank in the scent of him.

The room was nearly pitch-dark, and she couldn't remember the last time she'd felt so satisfied—if ever. It felt marvelous to be in his arms, to draw on the strength of his powerful body. For the first time in years, she didn't feel alone.

"What did you want to tell me about the call?"

"Barbara is looking for me."

"For you?" Haley asked as she nestled in the crook of his arm. "Too bad, I got here first."

"My ego thanks you."

"It should. I don't exactly sleep around."

"I figured that out all by myself," Dalton said as he kissed the top of her head. "But I should probably call Barbara and see what she wants. The message said it was urgent."

Haley smacked his chest as she scrambled to her feet, grabbing her robe in the process. "Maybe she's heard from Claire. I can't believe you didn't say something before we..."

"Which is exactly why I didn't say anything."

"You are a pig," Haley said, only half-teasing. "I can't believe you are so selfish."

"I wasn't being any more selfish than my willing partner."

"I hate you," Haley breathed as she dialed Barbara's number.

"Really?" he asked as he nuzzled her neck and slipped his hand inside her robe. "Really?"

Giggling, Haley finally said "No," just as Barbara picked up the phone.

"You aren't going to believe this," Barbara said excitedly. "Guess who just called here looking for Claire?"

"Greg Beater-of-women Walsh?"

"Nope, Justin. Obviously prison didn't cure him of terminal stupidity. He left a number."

Chapter Twelve

I care about you.

"He can't care about me because he doesn't know me."

He knows you intimately now.

"Only because I have no willpower," Haley argued with her little voice as she stood at the railing watching the morning sun spill over the Atlantic.

I care about you.

"I can't believe I fell for moonbeams and magic."

"At least you're willing to acknowledge there *was* a little magic involved."

Haley turned to find Dalton standing on the porch, clad only in his slacks and the sexiest sleep-laden smile she'd ever seen. "How long have you been standing there?"

"Long enough to know that you've got a mean case of the morning-afters."

Holding the edges of her robe close to her throat,

Haley couldn't meet his eyes. "I suppose I owe you an apology."

"For what?"

"For last night. It wasn't a very good idea. For either of us."

She tried to make a quick exit but he was having none of it. Using his large body, he blocked the entrance, probably knowing full well that she wouldn't touch him for anything.

"Please move."

"As soon as we finish this discussion."

"There's nothing to discuss and we need to get back to town to talk to Justin."

"He's not going anywhere. There's a unit watching the motel on Route 17. They'll radio if he decides to change locations."

Dropping her head forward, Haley sighed and resigned herself to the inevitable. "If you really feel a postmortem is necessary..."

"What I really wanted was for you to fling yourself into my arms and then we could have started the day off right."

Haley shifted on her bare feet, feeling as uncomfortable as a child awaiting punishment. Gathering what little strength she had, she looked up at him. Seeing the flicker of genuine disappointment in his eyes didn't make her feel much better. "It wouldn't be fair to you for us to start anything."

"We already started," he countered with a definite edge.

"We both got caught up in the situation," Haley reasoned. "We've been spending an incredible amount of time together. We're both healthy adults. It was understandable, but it can't work. We want different things."

"Nice speech," he ground out. "Sounds rehearsed. Do you give it often?"

She reacted by slapping his face. "Go to hell," she said, seething. "I was trying to be diplomatic."

"You aren't in a courtroom, Haley. Stop trying to make an argument."

Her palm stung and she noticed the outline of her hand beginning to appear on his freshly shaven cheek. She would have been contrite except she couldn't get that emotion past his arrogant, all-knowing smirk. "And this isn't a precinct, either, so stop giving orders. I don't have to explain myself to you. I just want to make it perfectly clear that what happened last night *won't* happen again."

"Want to bet?"

"You'd lose, Dalton," she told him as she pushed past him into the house.

"No, I won't. I don't lose, Haley!" he called after her as she raced up the stairs.

She took her time getting dressed, and when she joined him in the living room nearly an hour later, she fully expected to find him sulking like the wounded dog that he was. Instead, he was in the kitchen, whistling away as he heated water for instant coffee.

"Finished pouting?" he asked.

"I don't pout."

"You weren't putting on makeup," he remarked casually as he turned and let his eyes roam from her head to where her toes peeked out of her sandals.

"Sorry, but I don't carry around the whole cosmetics counter in my purse."

He shrugged. "Doesn't matter to me. I think you're beautiful."

"I think you're a jerk."

"No, you don't. You just can't admit that you like me yet. You will, eventually. People don't share the kind of intimacy we shared without—"

"Put a sock in it," she interrupted. "Can we please leave?"

"As soon as I have some coffee. You know cops, we can't function without caffeine and doughnuts."

He's making jokes! He thinks this is funny, does he? Haley fell into one of the chairs and crossed her arms over her chest.

"I don't suppose you have a newspaper delivered out here?"

"No."

Dalton sat down and sipped the coffee, grimacing as he swallowed. "This is nothing like the stuff you have back in Charleston."

"What is a two-year-old jar of instant coffee *supposed* to taste like?" she returned smartly.

He dumped the remainder in the sink, rinsed the dishes and finally announced he was ready to go. Grudgingly, Haley followed him out of the house, setting the alarm as she went.

"Why did you buy that house if you like living in the city?"

"I didn't buy it, my parents did."

"Why don't you spend more time here? It's got a killer view."

"Because I've been working and I feel isolated in that house."

"Why?"

Haley tightened her grip on her purse and kept her eyes fixed ahead in the road. "Why are you asking me so many questions?"

"It's called getting to know you."

"It's called a waste of time," she grumbled.

"You know," he began as his hand came to rest on her knee, "if you continue to act like a spoiled child, I'll have to punish you."

Haley snorted. "I don't think so."

Dalton veered the car off onto the shoulder of the road. Luckily it was early enough that there was no traffic on Kiawah Island Parkway. Haley opened her mouth to tell him exactly what she thought of his silly macho display when she was silenced by his kiss.

It wasn't just a kiss either. She refused to respond, calling on her full reservoir of control to keep from swooning as he gently held her face in his hands. Her lips remained a tight, straight line when he teased the seam with his tongue.

Lifting her hands to his chest, she had every intention of shoving him back where he belonged. Instead, the instant she felt the rapid beat of his heart beneath the wall of muscle and soft, downy hair, she was lost. Her brain took her back to last night, to the memories of how perfect it had been with him.

The next minute she was a willing, almost demanding participant. Her stomach coiled and her hands balled with fistfuls of his shirt. All the passion and desire she had ever known threatened to consume her as she tasted the coffee and mint on his breath.

And then came the blare of a car horn.

"We are the most interrupted couple I know," Dalton grumbled as he put the car into gear and waved to the driver behind them.

"We are not a couple."

He chuckled. It was a deep, rich sound that resonated through the car. "You like the term *lovers* better?"

"Eat dirt and die."

Masculine laughter was his only response.

"I'M SURPRISED to see you here," Dalton said as he walked up to the police vehicle parked beside a convenience store across from the motel where Justin Benedict was registered under an alias.

"I need the overtime," Sergeant Lauer answered. "If you can find ex-wife number two a new husband, maybe I wouldn't have to spend so many nights eating stale doughnuts and OD'ing on coffee."

Dalton smiled. He'd worked his share of stakeouts. They were boring, uncomfortable and not the kind of duty most officers volunteered for. Unless you're buried under a couple of divorces, he thought.

Leaning against the car's window frame, he saw his own face reflected in Lauer's mirrored sunglasses. "I was wondering if you remembered any more about popping this guy's wife for possession."

"Naw," Lauer answered quickly. "I've been arresting people for twenty-five years, the past twelve in narcotics. After that long, they all kinda run together."

"Mind getting me a copy of your notes on the bust?"

Dalton recognized that the small muscles around the sergeant's mouth twitched ever so slightly before he said, "Sure. I'll do it first chance."

Dalton placed his hand on the man's shoulder and said, "Thanks. Why don't you call it a morning."

"Don't you want me to stick around for backup?"

"No need," Dalton answered. "This guy has no history of violence."

"But he's an ex-con," Lauer argued. "And who's the woman in your car?"

"An attorney. I wouldn't want to violate any of Mr. Benedict's constitutional rights."

Lauer and Dalton shared a laugh before the slightly rotund officer drove away. Dalton's smile faded as soon as the police car disappeared from his sight. He needed coffee.

"I'll be right back," he told Haley, leaving without waiting to hear her voice a complaint.

Inside the convenience store, Dalton got two jumbo coffees and waited his turn behind a boisterous group of construction workers. He sighed heavily, as he replayed the scene with Lauer in his brain. Something was wrong, that much he knew. He didn't know Lauer well. The man's record had checked out. "Haley's conspiracy-around-every-corner mind-set must be getting to me," he mumbled as his eyes drifted to her.

She had the unique ability to take his breath away. He couldn't look at her face without remembering vividly how it had been last night. So she thought it was a mistake, huh? Well, he could be patient. At least he hoped he could.

"Thanks," she grumbled as he handed her a plastic-foam cup. "Are we going to spend all day in the parking lot?"

He gave her a sidelong glance. "Are you always this grumpy in the morning?"

"I am not grumpy. I just don't want Justin to get away before we find out what he did with Claire."

Dalton took a sip of his coffee. "You're assuming he did something. Aren't you folks always reminding the world that a person is presumed innocent until proved guilty?"

"Stop lumping me with all your negative stereotypes of attorneys. I've never represented a criminal defendant."

"Deal," he agreed easily. "If you'll stop treating me like I'm a reincarnation of Cal."

"Who told you about that?" she demanded. "Besides, incidentally, I am doing no such thing. Cal was killed a long time ago, not that I think it is any of your business. But I'm not some pathetic woman who can't deal with tragedy."

"I didn't say you were pathetic. I was simply asking that you keep an open mind."

"I have an open mind."

"Then why are you screaming at me?"

"Because I don't like the idea that you've been snooping around. I'm not the one missing, Claire is."

"But you *are* the one getting stabbed and having your picture taken."

"In the future, I would appreciate it if you would ask *me* if you want to know something."

Nodding, Dalton said, "If you insist."

Crossing the busy highway, he pulled the car into a spot near the only stairway leading to the second floor. "Maybe it would be best if you stayed behind," he suggested. Her response was predictable.

"No way," she said as she bounded from the car.

Uttering a string of expletives, he chased after her. "We don't know what's waiting for us," he called. "Let me go first." He delivered the last line while grabbing her arm and giving her a sharp tug.

Reluctantly, Haley fell back behind him. Shielding her with his body, Dalton reached in and flicked open the snap on his holster. The curtains were drawn, so he placed his ear against the door. The muffled sound of the television was blended with occasional laughter.

Dalton pulled out his service revolver. Then, rearing back, he kicked the door in, splintering the frame in the process. "Don't move!"

The man on the bed looked at him with fear and surprise in his eyes. It wasn't until his attention went to Haley that the transformation occurred. The man glared at her with what could only be described as pure hatred.

"What is this all about?"

"Nice to see *you* again, too," Haley answered. "You put on a little weight in prison, Justin."

Moving to the bed, Dalton yanked Justin to his feet, then searched his jeans for weapons. Satisfied that the guy was clean, he shoved him back onto the unmade bed, then turned off the television.

"You a cop?" Justin asked.

"Detective Ross." Dalton flashed his shield. "How have you been, Justin?" he asked as he stood at the end of the bed. "Your parole officer is wondering why you aren't in the apartment you rented. You can't move without informing them."

Justin seemed to blanch and small beads of perspiration began to gather in the stubble above his upper lip. "I don't know what that bit—"

"Don't go there, Justin. You really don't want to make me angry," he warned. "Now, tell me about Claire."

"Why is *she* here?" he hissed.

"Because I know you're responsible for whatever's happened to Claire."

Justin snorted. "Nice try, Haley."

Dalton noted that the man used her name like some sort of vile curse. He was every negative thing Barbara had told him and more. Justin had that hangdog look that some women seemed go for.

"We're going to have a little conversation," Dalton began, just as a frantic older man appeared at the door.

"I warned you—no trouble at my place," he rasped.

Dalton showed the man his badge. "The department will cover the damage."

The man reluctantly nodded. "What am I supposed to do until I can get this door fixed?"

"I'll deal with you later, sir," Dalton said. "Now, where were we?"

Justin sat up as soon as the manager had left. "You're going to get me thrown out of here."

Dalton looked around the shabby room and shrugged. "I can call your parole officer and make arrangements for you to become a guest of the city again."

"Wait," Justin nearly shouted. "I haven't done anything. I swear."

"Then why don't you explain why you disappeared?" Haley suggested. "Or better still, tell the detective where we can find Claire."

Justin shook his head, then raked slightly shaking hands through his longish hair. "I know you think I'm a sleaze, Haley, but—"

"An impartial jury thought you were, too," Haley shot back.

Dalton looked over to gauge the fire in her eyes. If he thought Justin hated Haley, there wasn't a word in the English language to describe what he saw in her expression. "I'm not here to chat about old times, Justin." He paused and gave Haley a warning look as well. "If you can't satisfy my curiosity, I won't have any option other than to take you in."

"For what?" Justin bellowed. "I haven't done anything!"

"Then why did you run?" Dalton asked. Justin

stood and paced in the small area Dalton would allow. The guy was definitely wired. "I'm waiting."

"It isn't wh-what you think," he stammered.

"Really?" Dalton barked. "Then get on with an explanation because I'm running really low on patience."

"Okay," Justin breathed as he threw up his arms. "I ran because I was scared."

"What have you done?" Haley asked. Anxiety made her voice quiver. "Please tell me what you did to Claire."

"You have it all wrong," Justin began, head hung and speaking to the floor.

Dalton put away his gun and asked, "What do we have wrong?"

"I haven't hurt Claire. I was helping her."

"Helping her what?"

"She needed the name of a guy I heard about in prison."

"What kind of guy?" Dalton asked.

"An investigator. Stan Jackson has a reputation for digging hard. A lot of the white-collar guys used him to get dirt on their wives or their business partners while they were stuck behind bars."

"I didn't think there were any bars in that country club they sent you to," Haley sneered.

"It might have been minimum security, but it was still prison, Haley. Trust me."

"Trust you? You're a thief."

Justin looked to Dalton, silent pleading in his tired eyes.

"Who did you connect her with?"

"National Investigative Services in Baltimore."

Dalton and Haley exchanged a brief glance. Then Dalton asked, "What was Claire having investigated?"

"That doctor. The one that filled her full of all that crap about sperm donors."

"Dr. Tate?" Haley asked.

Justin shook his head. "Not him, the new guy she was seeing."

"Dixon?" Dalton asked.

"Right, Dixon," Justin said. "I don't know why she was going to give him all that money when I told her I was more than willing to father her child."

Haley groaned. "She wanted to have a baby, Justin, not a little slimeball that would someday grow into a big slimeball."

Justin's boyish face hardened. "Has it dawned on you that this is all your fault?"

"Right, Justin. I made you steal money from Claire."

"If you hadn't convinced her to file charges, we could have worked things out," Justin insisted. "We would still be married and she would never have gotten involved with that doctor."

"Hold on," Dalton said. "Claire wasn't involved

with Dr. Dixon. She missed her appointment the day she disappeared.''

Justin shook his head vehemently. "She met him. He called her to ask about her questionnaire.''

"What are you babbling about?''

"Claire called me all upset because Dr. Dixon had found out about me. About my conviction.''

"So?" Haley remarked.

"So Claire calls and—''

"When was this?" Dalton interrupted.

"About a week before she disappeared. She calls and says this doctor had run a background check on her. She was miffed. That's when she asked me about the investigator and...''

"And what?''

Lowering his eyes, Justin said, "She told me I had to provide her with an affidavit.''

"What sort of affidavit?" Haley asked.

"She said Dr. Dixon refused to continue treating her if we were sleeping together.''

"You can do better than that," Haley scoffed. "Why would a reputable doctor want an affidavit from a lowlife like you? And, on the incredibly small chance that you're telling the truth for the first time in your life, why would Claire come to you instead of Barbara or me?''

Justin shrugged. "I only know what she told me.''

"Which was?" Dalton prompted.

"She said that if she was wrong, it would cost Haley her job.''

Chapter Thirteen

"He's got to be lying," she told him again as they climbed the steps to her house. "It doesn't make any sense that Claire would turn to Justin and not one of us."

"What about the night she disappeared?" Dalton asked. "Wasn't the dinner her idea?"

Haley nodded as she opened the front door and let out a small gasp.

"What?" Dalton called as he pulled her against him with one arm. His other hand held a gun.

She was acutely aware of his hard body pressed against her own. It was as if every one of her cells carried the sweet memory of his touch to her brain. Even fully clothed, Haley could easily forget her principles. All she had to do was close her eyes and remember.

"I don't see anything out of the ordinary," Dalton said softly. His breath washed over her ear, down across the exposed skin of her neck.

"There's no mess," she managed in a near whisper. The desire to turn around and seek pleasure in his arms was almost overwhelming.

"Does that mean Malcolm and his pals are gone for good?" he asked in a suggestively low tone.

Before she could answer, Dalton had holstered his gun and pulled her to him. She needed to summon the litany of objections. This was craziness. Pure lunacy to allow it to happen again. Still, what was the harm in just letting him hold her?

"I guess," he said as he began placing feathery kisses on her throat, "this means...we're...alone."

A tight coil of desire spread from where his lips brushed her flushed skin down into the core of her now-trembling body. Her legs actually felt weak as she arched backward, allowing his mouth to work its subtle magic. Just a few more seconds, she promised herself.

"You have the softest skin," he murmured.

"Dalton." She sighed his name. It was part swoon and part weak objection.

His fingers gripped her waist. "I'm guessing you're about to tell me to stop." There was sadness, tinged with a healthy dose of disappointment, in his voice.

"We can't keep doing this."

"But you said we were both healthy, consenting adults."

"Consenting adults with no future."

Haley stepped out of his embrace. She wasn't sure whether she was flattered by the fact that he hadn't belabored the point, or sorry that he hadn't pressed the issue.

A few minutes later, in the safety of her bedroom, Haley felt her heart still racing. "I'm losing my mind," she chided softly. "Only a real idiot would begin an affair with a man in the middle of a major life crisis."

As she stripped off her clothing, her thoughts volleyed back and forth between reason and her irrational, uncharacteristic response to the man. As the tub filled with hot water, she watched the steam rise without really seeing it. "I should be totally focused on finding Claire and instead I'm lusting after a man I don't want."

She laughed without humor. "Okay, so I want him in that way," she grumbled. "Who wouldn't? The man is gorgeous. He can be funny, charming, protective, even jealous. He can also be gunned down one night in some alley."

The bath helped her relax, and by the time she had finished drying her hair, her determination to keep their relations strictly professional was clear in her mind. Her heart was another matter. Somewhere along the way she had started to fall for him. It was the only way she could have made love with him with such complete and total abandon. Well, she would just have to make sure the course of their budding relationship changed before she made a mess of her life and his.

"This really has taken shape," Dalton remarked as she joined him in the dining room.

The way he looked at her, with unmasked admiration in his eyes, put the first chink in her newly donned armor.

"I'm finally to the point where they do the painting and the finish work," Haley answered, forcing her tone to remain light.

"I guess you spent all that time upstairs convincing yourself to keep your distance," he remarked with a rueful smile.

Haley lowered her eyes. "I really don't want to beat this horse to death. It won't work and we'll both end up losing if we keep letting our hormones get the better of our brains."

"Why would that be so awful?" he asked gently as he came to her, gripping her arms. "Why are you so afraid of what's between us?"

Haley shrugged away from him and went to the window. "There isn't anything between us except a lot of chemistry."

"I don't know about you," Dalton argued, "but I've never felt this way before. You can call it chemistry, but I think it's more than that. I think it's—"

She cut him off by turning and placing her finger against his lips before he could utter the word. "Please?" she asked softly, meeting his eyes.

"Don't make this difficult for me. I won't lie about how much I like being with you, but I won't lie about the rest either. I'm not what you're looking for, Dalton. And you sure aren't what I want. Why start something that will only end badly?"

"Are you psychic, too?" he asked with a harshness that had the same effect as if he'd yelled.

"I don't have to be psychic. I only have to know what I feel in my heart. Incredible sex would never be enough to make up for all the things we don't have." *Like security. Like saying forever and meaning it.*

He looked at her with so much pain and longing Haley almost caved in. It was only the memory of how much it had hurt when the police chaplain had come knocking all those years ago that allowed her to stand firm.

"What if incredible sex was enough for me?"

"It isn't enough for me," Haley told him. "I'm really sorry."

"So am I," he said as his fingers reached out and cupped her cheek. "Because I can't promise that I won't keep trying."

Haley lowered her lashes and drew her bottom lip between her teeth. "It won't change the way I feel."

"We'll see."

"NICE DIGS," Dalton said as he held open the door to Dr. Dixon's Women's Health Center. "I wonder how many artificial babies he has to make to keep this place going.''

"The babies aren't artificial," Haley whispered. "Some of us don't have the luxury of waiting around for Mr. Right.''

Dalton touched her arm, halting her in midstep. Bending his head, he whispered, "Speaking of which, we didn't exactly practice responsible sex last night."

Haley felt her face flame. "Don't worry. You're safe."

"Am I?"

She jerked away from him and almost ran up to the semicircular desk manned by a bank of women. If the incessant ringing of the telephone were any indication, their chances of getting an audience with the doctor were somewhere between slim and none.

"Good afternoon. May I have your name please?"

"I'm Detective Ross," Dalton answered as he produced his badge for the young woman's inspection. "I need to speak to Dr. Dixon."

The woman, along with her four co-workers, seemed surprised. "I'm afraid the doctor has a full afternoon. Perhaps you'd like to make an appointment for—"

"Perhaps you should buzz your boss and ask him if he'd like to see me now or have me call downtown for a warrant."

"I'll handle this," said a woman Haley judged to

be somewhere in her late forties. "Wait over there and I'll speak with the doctor."

Haley and Dalton took seats in a small area to the left of the reception desk. They were the only people there.

"If this guy is so busy, why doesn't his waiting room look like Dr. Tate's?"

After glancing around, Haley said, "I think this is some sort of anteroom. Claire said this place was very discreet."

"Have you thought of any relation between Claire hiring that investigator and your job?"

"There isn't any," Haley answered. "Justin was probably lying."

"Why would he lie about the questionnaire?"

"Because for Justin, lying is the only form of communication he knows."

"I've spent almost twenty years as a cop, Haley. I would bet my pension on my belief that Justin was on the up-and-up."

"Then I hope you've got a backup for your old age."

"Detective?"

They both stood as the woman called his name from where she stood holding open one of three doors in the anteroom.

It was apparent from her body language as well as her tightly pursed lips that she wasn't exactly welcoming Haley and Dalton with open arms. Her white shoes squished as she led them down a narrow corridor. Everything was decorated in pastels. Right down to the pink-and-blue checkered tiles on the floor.

"Dr. Dixon will give you five minutes between patients. Wait in here."

"Thank you," Dalton said.

When she closed the door and left them in an examining room, Haley let out a breath. "She could use a little personality transplant."

"She's probably just miffed because we're disturbing Dr. God."

She cocked one brow and asked, "Are you indicting the doctor because his nurse is a witch?"

"Let's just say I have a very strong feeling that Michael Dixon, M.D. will be one of those types that thinks he's a cut above the rest of us."

"He gives people a chance to have children, Dalton. That is an incredible vocation."

"Except, unlike God, he gets a pretty hefty paycheck for his miracles."

When the doctor appeared, he had neither horns nor a pitchfork. In fact, Haley liked him almost at once. His smile was reassuring and he made a point of apologizing for the delay as he shook her hand.

"Lisa said you were from the police?"

Dalton gave Haley a guarded look before he answered and again displayed his shield. "I was hoping you could give me some information about Claire Benedict.''

''I'm afraid that name doesn't ring a bell.''

''She was referred to you by Dr. Tate. Her appointment was a couple of weeks ago.''

The doctor's eyes brightened and he bobbed his head. ''She never kept her appointment,'' he said as he turned and grasped the door handle. ''I'm sorry you wasted a trip out here. A phone call to my office would have saved us both some time.''

Dalton's hand grabbed the door, preventing the doctor from making an exit. ''I would like to look at Ms. Benedict's file.''

This seemed to rattle the physician. ''What exactly are you interested in?''

''The file might provide a lead as to Ms. Benedict's current whereabouts.''

''Yes,'' Dixon said. ''I recall reading something about her being missing.''

''Which is why I need to see that file.''

Dixon reached up and gently but firmly brushed Dalton's hand aside. ''I know there is nothing in my file that could help you.''

''I'd like to judge that for myself.''

''As much as I would like to cooperate, patient privilege would prevent me from revealing anything,'' Dixon said.

''Privilege can be waived,'' Haley said.

The comment earned her a rather stern look from

the doctor. "Only by Ms. Benedict," he said rather triumphantly. "I really must go now, I have people waiting. Besides, I didn't treat Claire Benedict. Perhaps you should speak to Dr. Tate."

When they left the building, Haley could no longer contain her smile.

"You seem pretty happy, considering the fact that we just got blown off. In case you don't know it, I don't have any probable cause for a warrant. The nurse bought my bluff, but Dixon won't."

"Forget what Dixon did or didn't buy."

"Why?"

Haley grabbed the sleeve of his shirt and looked up into his eyes. "If we go to my office so I can get what I need to prepare a motion, we should be able to break through Dixon's defensive line by tomorrow at the latest."

"You lost me."

"I'll have a judge declare Claire incapacitated by reason of her unexplained absence. I'll need you available to testify."

"Why are we having her declared incompetent?"

"To toss Dr. Dixon's privilege back at him."

"I still don't follow."

Playfully, Haley grabbed his tie and pulled his face down toward her level. "If Claire is incapacitated, her guardian can waive privilege."

"But doesn't it take a while to get the court to appoint a guardian?"

"Usually, but I happen to hold power of attorney in this situation."

Dalton's mouth curved into a slow, sexy grin. "The judge rules and you have control over her medical records?"

"Very good, Detective."

"You," he began as he lifted her off the ground and kissed her squarely on the lips, "are brilliant."

"Ms. JENKINS?" Betterman said as she stepped off the elevator with Dalton on her heels.

"Don't worry," she said politely. "I'm only here to use one of the forms I keep on my PC."

"Your PC?" her possibly-former boss asked.

"Her résumé," Dalton said as he gripped her elbow and held the elevator door for Betterman.

"Please forgive the detective," Haley said. "His sense of humor is sometimes poorly timed. It has nothing to do with my résumé, sir."

"Perhaps I should come with you and—"

"Don't worry," Dalton cut in. "I'll make sure she doesn't steal any paper clips."

The doors closed on a very flustered Betterman. "You shouldn't have done that," Haley chided. "I *was* hoping to get my job back once we find Claire."

"Judging by the way everyone is staring at you, I wouldn't hold my breath."

He was right. The people she had called friends just two short weeks ago now peered out at her from barely cracked doors. Those unlucky enough to have no private office to hide in were forced to lower their eyes and feign activity as she passed.

"How are you?" Roxanne asked, though she didn't offer the greeting until she had looked around to make sure no one else would see her speaking to the pariah.

"I'm fine," Haley assured her. "I hope they're keeping you busy while I'm out."

"Mr. Phelps is going to transfer me to the corporate division," Roxanne said. "What are you doing here? I thought... They sorta indicated that you wouldn't be back."

"Don't worry," Haley said as she struggled to smile at Roxanne. "Everything will work out for the best."

"Do you think I'll like corporate? It sounds really boring, but they gave me a raise and guarantee that I can have off every school holiday."

"That's great, Rox. I'm sure it will be good for you."

"I think I hear taps playing," Dalton said as soon as she closed the door. "I wonder when they were going to get around to telling you."

Haley put a diskette into her computer and copied the legal motion. She turned to a filing cabinet and opened one drawer, then another.

"I can't believe this," she fumed. "My files are all gone."

She confronted her secretary. "Roxanne! That bastard Phelps insisted that they weren't firing me." Haley copied the motion to disk and put it in her purse. "I can't believe this!" she fumed. "My files are all gone. Roxanne!"

"Yes, Ms. Jenkins?"

"Where are my files?"

"Mr. Phelps had all your cases reassigned."

"Not my open case files. My personal files."

"I think they sent them down to the basement for storage."

"Great!" Haley snapped. Then, turning to Dalton, she said, "C'mon. This could take forever."

"You took your coffee cup and your diploma and you left your personal files here?" Dalton asked as they stepped into the elevator.

"I thought they'd be safer here. I also thought I'd be coming back."

"What is this place?" he asked when the doors opened.

"We call it the dungeon. It's where we keep old files, closed cases, that sort of thing."

"So where do we start?"

"You take the filing cabinets, I'll take those boxes."

Haley pointed to a small row of silver-gray cabinets divided alphabetically, while she moved to a tower of cardboard boxes labeled with handwritten indexes. "The cabinets should have dates on them. Start with the newer stuff and work backward."

"What am I looking for?" Dalton called.

"Files marked Jenkins. My power of attorney for Claire is in one of those files."

The first three stacks were all exhibits from one of the longer, more protracted insurance cases Jonathan Phelps had handled recently. The mere thought of that lying weasel inspired her indignation. He must have known they were going to fire her, yet he had sat in that chair and lied through his capped teeth.

"Maybe when this is over, I'll sue this firm."

"For what?"

"I'll think of something," she assured Dalton.

"I've been through the recent files. Want me to keep working backward?"

"Sure, they probably buried my stuff down here out of spite."

"Who is L.B.3?" Dalton called.

"Probably Betterman—as in Lawrence Betterman III. Someone's idea of an innovative storage system. Why?"

Haley received no response and she was about to ask again when she found the box she was looking for. "Got it!"

Tossing off the box top, she checked the contents till she was satisfied that everything that had been in the locked cabinet in her office was present and accounted for. "Dalton!" she called. "C'mon, I found what I needed."

When he emerged from between two rows of file cabinets, he looked troubled.

"What?"

"Probably nothing," he said, the jovial expression returned to his handsome face. "Do you want to do the motion here?"

Haley shook her head. "I'll use the computer at Claire's house."

"You don't have one of your own?"

"Not one as fast as Claire's, and her place is on the way to the courthouse."

"Very efficient, Ms. Jenkins."

"Not bad for an unemployed lawyer."

"You haven't been fired yet."

She gave him a sidelong glance. "I heard taps, too."

It took them just a few minutes to get to Claire's home. Haley experienced a small shiver as she stepped across the threshold. "I can't believe she's been gone for so long."

Dalton draped his arm across her shoulder. "I hope we can find her in time."

"That wasn't very comforting."

"I just don't want you to—"

"Thanks," she said as she sat at the computer and flipped the switch. "I know she might be dead, Dalton. But I choose to believe otherwise."

"Fair enough." He sighed.

As her fingers flew across the keys, she was aware of Dalton moving around the room. If she hadn't written this type of motion a few hundred times, it would have been an impossible task. His agility was at definite odds with his size. All that hard muscle tempered by all that grace. It was a heady mixture, one that made her feel a pang of regret. He was so sexy, so appealing. Why did he have to be a cop?

"You must be desperate," she teased when she saw him flipping through the manual for Claire's fax machine. "I'm sure there's a cereal box in the kitchen. I won't be much longer."

Dalton wasn't paying her a bit of attention. Curious, Haley swiveled in the seat while the computer formatted her motion. He pressed a few buttons on the fax machine, referring occasionally to the manual as he worked.

"What are you doing?"

"Just checking something."

"Barbara already printed the journal from that machine."

"She printed the records of the faxes received. I'm checking to see what Claire sent." The machine came to life, spewing a lot of paper before it let out an annoying beep.

"Anything interesting?" Haley asked.

Dalton gave her a bright smile. "When you get

your hands on Dixon's records, make sure you check the week before Claire disappeared.''

"Why?''

"She sent him two transmissions that day.''

"The questionnaire?'' Haley suggested.

"Whatever it was, it took eleven pages.''

"Probably the questionnaire then.''

"She also sent him three others in the days before she vanished.''

Haley took the paper from him, scanning the list of numbers. "She wasn't just talking to Dixon. This one—'' she paused and pointed to one near the top "—was sent to my firm.''

"Sounds like Mr. Phelps might have another reason for wanting you gone. Isn't Phelps Dixon's attorney?''

"Maybe Justin wasn't lying,'' Haley breathed. "Maybe Claire found out something about Dixon and Phelps and that's why she was worried about my job.''

"Maybe she found out something that made her a liability to one of them.''

"But neither one of them is a killer,'' Haley said.

Dalton brushed a kiss against her forehead and said, "That we know of.''

Chapter Fourteen

"It is the order of this court that Haley Jenkins be appointed interim guardian in re Claire Benedict."

The pounding of the gavel reverberated through a courtroom filled with hookers, drug addicts and pimps. Haley had decided to go home and change into a business suit before presenting her motion, which meant she had no choice but to make her request at night court.

"Thank you, Your Honor."

"The court hopes your friend is found soon," he said, giving her a kind smile.

Haley returned the gesture before she packed up her briefcase and went to the clerk of court to wait for the printed ruling. It took the clerk only five minutes to fill out the form, but in that time three prostitutes were remanded to the detention center. Justice was swift in night court.

"Where did Dalton go?" she asked Barbara.

"He's getting the car. He suggested we all go back to the Rose Tattoo for some dinner."

Haley held her hand against her stomach. "I haven't eaten all day. He must be starved by now. But I'd rather go see Dixon first. I want those records."

Barbara's eyes shimmered devilishly as she hooked her arm through Haley's. "That sounded like you were more concerned with his welfare than your own."

"He's been running around with me since early morning," Haley explained, hoping to throw her friend off the topic. Then she told Barbara of their encounters with Justin and Dixon.

When they emerged from the building, Dalton was leaning against the car with the motor running. "We'll meet you at the restaurant," he said to Barbara.

"Don't worry, I wasn't going to tag along. Not now that Haley has *the look.*"

Dalton grinned as Haley elbowed her friend. "I hate you," Haley whispered. "I do not have any look."

Barbara clucked her tongue. "You do too. I think it's great. Keep it up, Dalton. She needs someone like you to break the monotony of her life."

"I'll break one of your legs if you don't close your mouth," Haley said, seething. "Go on, we'll be right behind you."

"No, we won't," Dalton said. Looking at Barbara he added, "She won't eat until she has Claire's records from the doctor. I'll take her over there now and we'll bring them back with us."

Barbara leaned close to Haley and said, "He reads your mind. A definite sign."

"Go away," Haley grumbled.

She couldn't look at Dalton as he drove. Not until she felt some of the heat drain from her face.

"There's nothing to be embarrassed about," he said after they had traveled a few miles in silence. "I can't help it if the way I feel about you is written all over my face."

"Barbara wasn't talking about your feelings, Dalton. And we won't, either."

"Yes, ma'am. But I would think you'd be a little nicer to me since I am ignoring near-fatal starvation to take you to the Women's Health Center."

"I do appreciate it," Haley said. "Really."

"Care to show me a little gratitude?" he teased as his hand covered hers. "I know a great little place where we could go parking."

Haley laughed in spite of herself. "Parking?"

"You know. We kiss and fondle and steam up the windows until some annoying cop comes along and interrupts us?"

"You are the annoying cop," she pointed out. "So we can just skip the kissing and fondling parts."

"You're no fun."

"I know. But something tells me that barging in on Dr. Dixon at nine p.m. will be a virtual riot."

"I think you're starting to like this stuff."

"I like the idea of finding my friend."

Luckily, lights burned from several floors of the four-story building. Unlike their first visit, they found the front doors locked. Dalton pressed a bell and it was a matter of seconds before a security guard came lumbering forward.

He wore an unwelcoming frown until Dalton pressed his identification to the glass.

"The Center is closed."

"Is Dr. Dixon here?" Dalton asked as he stuck his foot inside the partially open door.

"He doesn't see people this time of night," the guard responded as if by rote.

"This isn't a social call," Dalton growled. "Get him down here, now."

"I have strict instructions—"

"And I have the authority to arrest you for hindering a police official in the performance of his duties."

"Okay, okay."

Haley followed Dalton inside, her briefcase clutched against her side as if it contained the crown jewels. Again she and Dalton were assigned seats in the small anteroom.

"Relax," he said as he touched her arm. "We're the ones with the power here."

"I know." She sighed. "I think there's a part of me that is afraid of what this will lead to."

Dalton put his arm around her and rested her head against his shoulder. He smelled faintly of cologne and soap and the rough fabric of his jacket tickled her cheek.

"Don't ever be afraid of the truth."

"Very profound, Detective. Quoting one of the Great Masters?"

"Actually, it was in a fortune cookie."

"What do you think you're doing coming here in the middle of the night?" Dixon thundered as he made a grand entrance with the guard slinking in his wake.

Dalton rose slowly, taking Haley with him. "Miss Jenkins and I will take that file now."

A deep crimson stain began creeping up Dixon's throat. "I've already explained—"

"Here is an order from Judge Gannon," Haley said. "You'll see that I am now in a position to waive privilege on Claire's behalf. I do, so please provide Detective Ross with everything you have."

"This can't be right," Dixon muttered. "Stay here," he commanded as he disappeared back through the door.

"Ten bucks says he's calling Phelps," Dalton whispered.

"Ten more dollars says my career is definitely over."

"Don't worry, Haley. I'm sure you'll think of something else."

"I have," she said as the thought only then seemed to crystallize in her mind.

"You've come to your senses and decided to devote all your waking hours to making mad, passionate love with me?"

"No pay and definitely no benefits."

"Ouch," he quipped. "Seriously, what do you have in mind?"

"Wanda."

"Come again?"

"That woman in the trailer park. Girl, really. I'd bet she could use an attorney to make whoever fathered those babies pay some support."

"Maybe he does."

"If he does, then he isn't paying enough. That girl didn't even have a refrigerator. How will those children ever have a shot at life in that environment?"

"Careful, Haley, you may be jumping off the corporate ladder but I'm not sure you're ready to swim in the cesspool of reality."

"Thanks," she said as she met his eyes. "I'm not stupid, Dalton. I know it will be depressing, but no more so than going to bed every night knowing that there are children in my own community going without the basic necessities."

"I think—"

"Here," Dixon said as he tossed a file into Haley's lap. "Now, I have a procedure scheduled in a few minutes. If there's nothing else?"

Haley flipped through the folder and nothing jumped out at her. The questionnaire was there, as well as some other reports and notes.

"Is this the original?" Dalton asked.

"No. But you have my word that I personally copied every scrap of paper this office has."

"I think we just made an enemy," Haley remarked as they left the building. "But I've never yet met a doctor who liked having his records reviewed. Even the ones that don't have anything to hide."

"Does Dixon?"

"I'll know soon enough."

"YOU MEAN I sat in the scuzzy courtroom with all those crackheads for nothing?" Barbara cried.

"There's nothing here that even hints at what might have happened to Claire." Haley took a sip of her iced tea and continued her third reading of the documents. "Beside this very personal questionnaire, there's nothing that jumps out at me."

"Speaking of things that jump you," Barbara teased. "Dalton went upstairs to use the phone. He said he'd be right back."

"One more sexually explicit remark and you'll be wearing my dinner," Haley warned.

"Are you with him?" Susan asked, obviously pleased by the prospect.

"No."

"Yes," Barbara contradicted. "They've played house but Haley is trying her best to foul it all up."

"Why?" Susan asked. "He's so perfect for you. Madame Kerri told me that the two of you share the same alternate plane. Your souls walk together."

"Our futures are separate," Haley told her friends. "Now stop trying to marry us off, it isn't going to happen."

"And why not?" Rose demanded as she appeared at their table. "He *does* have a temper, but what passionate man doesn't?"

"What temper?" Haley asked.

"He was yelling so loudly that I had to leave my office. I'd sure hate to be the one on the other end of that phone." Rose fanned herself for effect. The action caused her necklace of panda bears holding hands to flutter. The matching earrings did the same, making it appear as if the little plastic animals were dancing to the Elvis tune playing in the background. "I think you should marry him. If I was a few years younger, I'd grab a man like him in a heartbeat."

"Grab away, Rose," Haley said. The minute the words left her mouth, she experienced the strangest sensation. Her mind kept seeing Dalton with a bevy of beautiful women. The mere thought of him doing to some other woman what he had done with her made her feel physically ill.

"You've gone pale, Haley," Susan said, concern etched into her face. "Did you find something?"

Yep, I found out that I'm in love with Dalton Ross. "No," she managed to answer.

"Then what's wrong?"

"I'm just tired," she lied. Then her eyes fixed on the metal tabs holding the pages in the file. Lifting the candle from the center of the table, she shone the light directly on the tabs.

"What are you doing?"

"Look at this," Haley said, a small hint of excitement returned to her voice. "Look at the creases in the metal."

"So?" Barbara asked.

"Watch when I close this." Haley bent the tabs back, then ran her finger along the clearly visible second seam. "Either Dixon recycled these tabs from another file, or—"

"Or he didn't copy every scrap of paper," Dalton finished for her.

"How do I go about proving that?" Haley asked.

Dalton shrugged and she noticed he had that same troubled look in his eyes she had seen earlier in the day. His body language was different too, as if he was nervous or agitated.

"Has something happened?" she asked in a panic. "Is it..."

"No, I'm just a little *miffed* at someone," he said,

apparently wishing to make light of whatever was bothering him.

"Should we go back to the Women's Center and see if Dixon will show us the original?"

"My guess is that he's already hidden, shredded or destroyed whatever was in there that he didn't want us to see."

"Like what?" Barbara asked.

"Like the background report on Claire."

"A credit check?" Barbara asked.

Haley shook her head. "According to Justin, the doctor had Claire checked out and dug up the fact that she wasn't widowed, as she lied on the questionnaire."

"I'd lie too if Justin was my ex-husband," Barbara snapped. "Why does a fertility specialist need a background check on a woman before he treats her?"

"Claire said he was discreet. Maybe he does it all the time," Haley suggested. "Maybe I'm making a mountain out of the proverbial molehill."

Dalton was about to say something when his cell phone chirped to life. Turning away from the table, he walked out on to the porch with the phone at his ear.

"What if *I* went to see Dr. Dixon?" Barbara suggested.

"What for?" Haley asked.

"I could pretend I wanted to do a campaign for

his Women's Center." Barbara seemed to grow more stimulated as she continued. "I'll be able to get into his office and hopefully, I could take a peek around."

"That's illegal," Haley reminded her. "Besides, Dalton would never allow it, nor would I. We don't know what this Dixon guy is up to, so promise me you won't do anything stupid."

Barbara hesitated.

"Please?" Susan and Haley said in unison.

"They're right," Rose added. "One missing girl at a time is one too many. Let Detective Ross do his job."

When Dalton returned he no longer looked troubled. In fact, he seemed almost happy as he strode across the room. Haley couldn't keep herself from silently admiring him. God, how was she going to keep saying no when every fiber of her body screamed yes?

"What?" Haley prompted.

"Finish your dinner, we have to go calling."

"Who are you going to see at this hour of the night?" Susan asked.

"We found Ray Anne Walsh. According to the motel clerk where she's staying, she isn't alone."

Chapter Fifteen

"This isn't like when we went to see Justin," Dalton said as he caught her by the hand. "Greg has a history of violence and I don't want you anywhere near him."

"But—"

He shook his head. "No, Haley. I've given you more latitude than I should have up to this point. This time is different."

Her lower lip protruded slightly, giving her a sexy, pouty look that could easily convince him to forget about his responsibilities. Whatever was waiting in that motel room could just wait a few minutes longer.

Dalton released her seatbelt and pulled her against him. She reached up to put her arms around him but he caught her hands and placed them against his chest. All the while their eyes locked. Maybe she wouldn't let him say the words, but he was determined to make her feel them.

He eased her mouth under his, glorying in her

sweet taste. She caressed him as he struggled to keep the kiss from becoming a demand. Her fingers teased a moan from his lips.

"Kiss me hard," she whispered achingly. "Please, Dalton?"

"In time," he promised as his palms urged her closer, trapping her hands. He lifted his head and took in the sight of her face. She was a vision of femininity, all fluttering long lashes and full, slightly red lips. He ached. "Haley, I'm only a man. I don't know if I have the strength to play this game with you."

"You're the one that suggested we go parking," she whispered as her fingers wound into his hair to pull him back to her. "Nothing more than this will happen, I promise," she whispered against his mouth.

He allowed the kiss to last a few more seconds before reluctantly lifting his head and letting a hard, heavy breath escape. "It just doesn't work this way." He sighed. "I don't think I can turn off at your whim."

"I wasn't trying to—"

Placing his finger against her lips, he managed a smile. "I know. I just want your word that you won't start something you don't intend to finish."

Haley shrank back against her seat and stared ahead. "I see. I'm sorry, Dalton. I should never have behaved this way. It would seem pretty foolish to deny that I want you, but it would never work with us."

He let out an exasperated breath and willed his body back to normal. "Never say never, Haley."

"More quotes from fortune cookies?"

"A friendly warning," he answered as he left the car.

He walked in the shadows of the first level of the battered motel. His strides were slow, purposeful. He had to rid his mind of this fixation on Haley. He couldn't burst through a door unless his mind and his body were working together. Damn, she was driving him nuts!

With his gun pointed down, he locked his elbows and leaned against the wall just to the left of room 107. Taking two deep breaths, he spun and kicked the door just above the knob. His action caused a woman to start screaming.

"Police!" Dalton called.

The woman cursed him and started to reach into a pile on the bed.

"Don't do it," Dalton warned. "Keep your hands where I can see them."

"My baby," she stammered.

Keeping his gun trained on the young brunette, he moved around the small room, using his peripheral vision to survey the place. "What's in there?"

The woman's brown eyes flickered with fear and indecision as her mouth opened but no response came. It was all he needed. Dalton reared back and kicked that door in as well. He almost rolled his eyes when he saw the thin man cowering in the shower. "Get up," he instructed. "Slowly and keep your hands where I can see them."

"I don't have any weapons," he insisted.

"Who the hell are you?" the woman yelped.

Dalton kept his gun poised as he chanced a glance toward the front door. "Damn it, Haley!"

She didn't even bother to look contrite. If anything, she looked anxious.

"You've been in here for a while and I didn't know what was happening," she said.

How could he be angry at her? She'd all but admitted that she'd come out of concern for his safety. "Check the bed," he said as he reached forward and caught the man by the shirt and dragged him out of the bathroom.

"There's a baby here," Haley said.

"Is he armed?" Dalton asked.

His smart remark earned him a short string of curses from the woman. "Calm down," Dalton barked. "Anything there beside the baby?" he asked Haley.

"No," she said as she lifted the fussy infant into her arms. "He's soaking wet."

"He's a she," the woman snapped. "Her name is Janette, and who gave you permission to hold my kid?"

Dalton tossed the man next to the woman and went to stand next to Haley. "Greg and Ray Anne Walsh?"

"We haven't done anything," Ray Anne snapped.

"Except child neglect," Haley grumbled. "Where are your things for the baby?"

Ray Anne snorted. "Social Services don't give me enough to make it till the first of the month."

Dalton held out his car keys to Haley. "There's a kit in my trunk with a few diapers and a can of something."

"Hey!" Ray Anne yelled. "She can't take my baby girl outta here without my permission."

"Then I'll arrest you and the baby will automatically become a ward of the state. Do you want Miss Jenkins to take care of your daughter, or would you rather have me call DSS?"

"Don't put up a fuss," Greg told his wife. "She's an attorney. A friend of Claire's."

"I'm supposed to feel better because your whore's friend has my baby?"

Dalton was glad Haley was out of earshot for that one. "Mrs. Walsh, either clean up your mouth or go to jail."

Ray Anne glared at him. "She'll behave herself," Greg said as he smacked the woman on the side of her head.

Dalton stepped forward and did the same to him,

only with a little more force. "Didn't your mother ever teach you not to hit women?"

"Don't you touch him!" Ray Anne yelled. "I'll file a complaint."

These people were pathetic. "Go right ahead, Ray Anne. You can file it from jail after I charge you with child neglect."

"You're only making it worse," Greg said. "Keep your foul mouth shut."

"Good advice, Greg," Dalton commented at the same time Haley returned. "The two of you have a seat on the bed. This is how it will work. I ask the questions and you give me the answers. If I don't like the answers, then you go to jail and the baby goes into foster care. Does everyone understand the rules?"

Ray Anne called him a colorful name under her breath. Greg elbowed her in the ribs. Dalton sighed heavily. "No name calling or hitting," he added. "Or we won't bother with the Q and A, we'll go right to the arrest part."

"What's all this about?" Greg asked. "I haven't done anything."

"Except beat Claire Benedict to a pulp," Haley said as she shifted the now-contented infant to her shoulder.

"She wouldn't leave Greg and me alone!" Ray Anne wailed.

"Try the other way around," Haley said to the

woman. "Your...*husband* was hounding her ever since they stopped seeing each other."

"If she said that, then she's a lying—"

"No name calling," Dalton reminded her. "Well, Greg, care to tell me *your* version of what happened?"

"I haven't seen Claire for almost three weeks."

That revelation earned him a hard shove from his wife.

"It wasn't like that!" Greg insisted. "Claire had this paper she wanted me to sign."

"An affidavit?" Haley asked.

Greg nodded. "She said she needed it for her doctor."

"Did you sign it?" Dalton asked.

Greg hung his head. "I was considering it."

Haley touched Dalton's sleeve and he met her eyes. "He's lying. Claire wanted a restraining order against him."

"Okay," Greg amended quickly. "I told Claire I would sign if she paid."

Dalton shook his head.

"That woman owed us," Ray Anne insisted. "She tried to take my man when I was having his kid."

"That would have been a real loss," Haley whispered. "How much was your signature going to cost?"

"Three grand," Greg answered. "But she double-crossed me."

"How?" Dalton asked.

"I met her and signed the paper, then she hands me a check. Only when I went to cash it, she had closed the account."

"I told you she was a—"

"Ray Anne," Dalton interrupted. "Your husband just confessed to a felony. Make me mad and I'll take him in now."

"What do you want from us?" Greg wailed.

"You were blackmailing Claire, and now she's disappeared."

"Hey!" Greg jumped to his feet. "She was fine when I left her."

"Like she was fine when you beat her last June?" Haley taunted.

"She was fine, I swear."

"Where did this little transaction take place?" Dalton asked.

"Just over the bridge. In the parking lot of some doctor's office."

"The Women's Health Center?" Haley asked.

"Yeah."

"What was the date?" Dalton asked.

"Couple of weeks ago," Greg answered. "It was early afternoon, a Thursday maybe."

"Was she alone?"

Greg's brows drew together for a minute, then he said, "Some guy met her at the door."

"What did he look like?"

"I don't remember."

"Try," Dalton growled.

"He was older, well-dressed. I only saw him for a second before they went inside."

"And you're sure about the date?"

"Here," Greg said as he fished out his wallet and pulled a crisply folded check from inside. "This has the date on it."

"Are we going to get our money?" Ray Anne asked.

"For now, just be grateful that I'm not busting you both. Haley, give them back the baby."

Ray Anne snatched the infant from Haley. The baby responded by letting out a sharp cry. Dalton had to take Haley by the hand to get her to abandon the child.

"After meeting Justin and Greg, I now understand why Claire would opt for artificial insemination."

He held the car door for Haley. "When it comes to men, all Claire's taste is in her mouth."

"So, any ideas about the man Greg saw with Claire? He's probably the last one to see her alive."

Dalton turned and saw the pale, stricken look on her face. Shutting his eyes, he winced. "I'm sorry, Haley. Force of habit. I didn't mean to imply that—"

"I know," she breathed. "But it's been almost three weeks."

"What about the man?"

"It could have been Dr. Dixon."

"Or someone closer to home."

Haley stared at him. "Like who? Greg couldn't have been describing Justin. If anything, he looks younger than his age."

"Closer to your home," he said as he drove away from the motel. "Or rather, your job."

Haley's eyed widened. "You can't possibly think that one of the partners is involved. What could they gain from doing harm to Claire? She makes the firm a lot of easy money."

"I'll work on that in the morning. I vote we both get a decent night's sleep."

"I don't know if I can sleep," Haley admitted.

Dalton said nothing until they reached her house. Taking her hand, he led her to the bedroom. "I know just the thing to relax you."

"We can't—"

He silenced her with a kiss that was meant to curl her toes. Minutes later, when he lifted his head, Haley no longer seemed to care about what they shouldn't be doing. Only what they were about to do.

"GREAT," Haley grumbled when she found Dalton's handwritten note taped to her coffee mug. She sighed, regretting the fact that she had spent the better part of an hour getting herself mentally prepared to tell Dalton that these trysts had to stop.

Malcolm and his crew came trickling in as she sat

at the table drinking her coffee and sulking like a child.

"Rough night?" Malcolm asked, pouring himself some coffee from the pot.

"Rough life," Haley answered flatly.

"That explains why there's still a cop car out front. They haven't caught the guy that stabbed you yet, huh?"

"They never will," Haley predicted.

"What about your friend?"

"He had an early-morning errand," Haley answered.

"Not him. That pretty lady friend of yours that's been missing."

"No luck, so far," Haley said as she jumped to her feet. "But you're right, Malcolm. I've got better things to do than sit here feeling sorry for myself."

"No need for depression, ma'am," Malcolm insisted. "We'll be done by the end of the week."

Haley smiled up at him. "Thank you. It really looks great."

"I'll be needing the final draw before then," he added. "I know you ain't working and all, but—"

"I'll write the check before I go out," she promised him.

"Much appreciated," Malcolm called after her. "If you need anything else done around here, y'all know who to call!"

"A Realtor," Haley muttered as she took the stairs two at a time.

After a shower, she selected a pair of linen shorts and a cotton top. Even though the calendar proclaimed fall was coming, she knew Charleston would be hotter than ever. Pulling her hair into a barrette, she put on sandals and reached for the telephone.

"Prather and Associates."

"Hi, this is Haley. Is Barbara available?"

"I'm so glad you called," Barbara's secretary gushed.

"What's wrong?"

"I can't find Barbara."

"What do you mean you can't find her?"

"She didn't come in this morning. She isn't answering her cell phone or her pager. I'm starting to get worried."

"Maybe she had a meeting," Haley suggested, trying to stem the tide of panic rolling through her stomach.

"No. She called me at home last night and told me to clear her appointments for this morning."

Haley relaxed a little. "Then she's probably getting a manicure or something. I'm sure she'll show up."

"I don't think so."

"Don't be silly," Haley said.

"I'm not. I'm telling you *something* is wrong."

"Barbara had you free up her morning for a reason." Haley tried to speak calmly. "She must have had something personal to attend to."

"Then why did she come in here during the night and take her portfolio?"

Chapter Sixteen

"I'm still waiting for that report," Dalton said to Sergeant Lauer when he found him in the break room of the precinct.

The officer brushed some powdered sugar off the front of his uniform. "Sorry, Ross. I forgot. I'll get to it first chance."

Taking one of the chairs and turning it backward, Dalton swung his leg over the chair and sat very close to the officer. "I'm still bothered about that collar," he said smoothly.

"What do you mean?"

Dalton shrugged. "I got blood work on the Benedict woman and she was clean."

"Maybe she did rehab," Lauer offered as he adjusted his tie. "Any luck finding her?"

"That's the weird part about this." Dalton sighed. "It's one of those cases that just doesn't add up, if you know what I mean."

Lauer began to perspire. "I've had a few of those

myself." He laughed nervously. "But, hey, we can't solve 'em all."

In a flash, Dalton grabbed the heavier man and slammed him against the closest wall. The other officers did nothing more than provide their full attention.

"Hey, Ross. What's your deal?"

"You're my problem, Lauer."

"That broad has gotten to you," he spit as Dalton tightened his hold on the man's shirt. "You've lost your objectivity. I heard there's even pictures of the two of you—uuumph."

"Sorry, my knee slipped," Dalton said.

"Ross? Is there a problem?" one of the men called.

"Not yet," Dalton called back without turning around. "We're going to have us a chat, Lauer."

Dalton took the man down the hall to an empty interrogation room. He tossed Lauer into one of the chairs. At least the man had the good sense not to try to get up.

"Now, tell me why a cop with a clean record who's only a couple of years away from his pension suddenly starts to falsify police reports."

Lauer squirmed in the chair, keeping his head bowed. "I don't know what you're talking about."

"I'll hurt you," Dalton warned. "Cop or not, I'll hurt you and then I'll hang your ass with Internal Affairs."

Lauer looked up, defeat in his eyes. "I swear, Ross. I only typed the report as a favor. I had no idea the woman would turn up missing when I did it."

"Nice try. You helped a kidnapper after the fact. You're looking at jail time for this."

"I swear," Lauer cried. "I typed that report weeks ago, before the Benedict woman disappeared."

"How many weeks ago?" Dalton asked.

"At least four," Lauer answered. "I swear."

"Betterman asked you to file a false report more than a month ago?"

Lauer went white. "It wasn't Betterman, it was his partner. Jonathan Phelps."

Dalton managed to hide his surprise. "But Betterman handled your first divorce," Dalton supplied. "Why did Phelps come to you?"

Raking his hands through his hair, Lauer let out a long sigh. "My second divorce cost me a bucketload of cash," he complained. "I was working my butt off trying to pay alimony, child support and the bills I owed two different attorneys. I was this close to living in the squad room." He pinched his thumb and forefinger together as punctuation.

"Phelps was the other attorney?"

Lauer shook his head. "A woman in Mt. Pleasant. She doesn't play into this."

"How did it go down?"

"Phelps said he could zero out my account with

Betterman if I made a drug bust appear for the Benedict woman. He gave me her information and a date for the arrest.''

"Did Phelps tell you why he wanted this done?''

"No. I figured she was probably married to a client of his and he was just trying to tip the scales in his favor.''

Dalton gave him a disgusted look and reached for the door.

"What are you going to do?'' Lauer asked.

"I'll let you know when I decide.''

"Is she still inside?'' Dalton asked the young officer he had placed in charge of Haley's safety.

"No one's come out. A few construction guys have gone in. I checked their IDs against the list you gave me.''

"Good work.''

"Something wrong?'' the young man asked.

Dalton didn't have an answer for that. He simply shrugged and dismissed the man. He still hadn't figured out how he was going to tell Haley that her boss was now the prime suspect.

"Afternoon, chief,'' Malcolm greeted as he looked up from his task of hammering some molding into place.

"Is Haley upstairs?''

Malcolm gave him a blank stare. "Haley?''

"The homeowner?'' Dalton said rather curtly.

"She left hours ago," Malcolm said. "Ran outta here like the devil was chasing her."

"Where did she go?"

"I don't know. Mumbled something about Barbara and Susan, then she slipped out through the alley."

Dalton ran from the house, cursing himself for not impounding her car. "I didn't think she'd be stupid enough to go out alone," he muttered as he jumped into his car and tore away from the curb, leaving the acrid smell of burned rubber in his wake.

With the help of his emergency lights, he made it to the Rose Tattoo in record time. He found the restaurant crowded as his eyes scanned the faces.

"She isn't here," Susan said as she came up to him. "Something terrible happened."

Dalton felt his stomach fall into his feet as he grabbed the waitress and dragged her into the kitchen so he could question her.

"What happened?"

"I don't know," Susan answered. "My crystal has been cold ever since I got her call. I knew something bad had happened."

"Please," Dalton begged as he gripped the woman's upper arms. "Don't feed me auras and crystals. I need to know what happened to Haley."

"Haley?" Susan parroted. "I thought you were talking about Barbara."

Dalton let his head fall back against the cool wall.

His hands dropped to his sides as he tried to process this new bit of information.

"Come upstairs," Susan said as she tugged at him.

Like a zombie, Dalton walked to the office and found Rose and Shelby at their respective desks. Rose spoke first. "No word from Barbara, either?"

"This defies logic," Shelby added. "I'm worried sick."

"Haley, too," Susan supplied.

"Sit down," Shelby instructed. "Susan, go downstairs and get the detective a drink."

"What the hell is happening around here?" Rose asked. "You don't think we have a serial killer loose, do you?"

Dalton wouldn't even entertain the thought that Haley was dead. "I'm pretty sure it has something to do with her firm."

"That bunch of frumpy lawyers?" Rose scoffed. "I don't know about the rest of them, but Betterman comes in here every few days shopping for the dumb blonde du jour. Do psychopaths usually go from lounge lizard to killer overnight?"

"Phelps is the key," Dalton said. "Maybe that's where Haley went. Maybe she stumbled onto something and went off to confront him."

"And where were you?" Rose fairly shouted. "How can you be in love with that girl and let this happen?"

"Good question," Dalton said as he stood.

"You are in love with her, aren't you?"

"Unfortunately," he admitted. "I hate to dash your hopes, Rose, but Haley doesn't love me."

"Maybe Haley is just afraid to love you."

"I can't worry about that until I find her."

"Where are you going?" Shelby asked.

"The law offices. I'll call when I know something."

He met Susan on the stairs, took the shot glass from her hand and tossed it back in one fortifying swallow. Then he went hunting.

THE GNATS WERE FEASTING on her legs and arms but Haley didn't dare swat them away. That might lead to detection and she was too close to risk giving herself away now. Not when she had spent the past five hours hidden in the bushes beneath a partially opened window.

As dusk slowly faded into night, Haley listened as the chorus of insects, those who weren't busy biting her flesh, became louder.

It was a good forty minutes later before she dared to stand, only to be crippled by cramps in her calves. She rubbed the tight muscles until normal feeling returned and she was able to get up on her toes to peer into the window.

The office was empty. No light emanated from the small crack at the base of the door. "It's now or never," she whispered as she struggled to push on the window, then held her breath for an alarm. Nothing.

Her arms ached as she pulled herself up on to the sill, then swung her legs inside, dropping soundlessly to the floor. Carefully, she lowered the window and allowed her eyes to adjust to the darkness.

With that accomplished, she went to the door. Slowly, she turned the knob. Even more slowly, she pulled just enough to allow one eye to peek out into the hallway. It was deserted. Haley shut the door.

Urged on by a small amount of confidence, she went to the desk and turned on the lamp. She was in the office of Cindy Wainsbrook. A quick search of the desk revealed that Miss Wainsbrook was some sort of genetic specialist. Haley moved to the filing cabinet, only to find it locked. Using the nail file from her small purse, she managed to break the lock. Her fingers instantly found a file with the name Claire Benedict neatly typed on the tab.

Taking the file to the desk, Haley began to read. Unfortunately, what she read made no sense. It was all some sort of complicated DNA study. The only part she understood was at the very end. Apparently Dr. Wainsbrook found Claire's DNA free from any known genetic defects.

Haley let out a breath. *Now what?*

Onward and upward, she decided. After checking the hallway and finding it clear, Haley tried each door as she passed. A few were locked and the ones that weren't turned out to be examination rooms much like the one she had visited with Dalton. Dr. Dixon's office door was closed and there was light spilling out from the bottom. Haley backtracked around a corner.

If Dixon caught her breaking into his building, Dalton would find out about it in a heartbeat. The mere thought of him made her flinch. He would be furious when he discovered what she was doing. *If I don't get myself killed by the security guard first.*

Barbara had to be here. She knew that because she had found her friend's car parked near the entrance to the parking lot. Haley had to swallow her fears and press on.

The elevator was too risky, so she followed the fire route and found a stairwell. The loud creak that sounded when she opened the door made her wince. She stood perfectly still for a few seconds, sure that she'd given herself away. Nothing.

Breathing easier, she slipped inside and discovered she had a choice. She decided to try the upper floors of the Women's Health Center. The second floor was a wash. It was nothing but a huge laboratory with shiny chrome machines, huge freezers and liquid nitrogen tanks. "Must be the sperm bank," she whispered.

The third and fourth floors were no help either. No locked doors, no secret rooms. That left the basement.

"I hate basements," she grumbled as she went back to the staircase and silently began her descent.

At the base of the stairwell, Haley found automatic double doors that opened from the other side. Cautiously, she looked through the small glass windows near the top of each door. She was looking out into what appeared to be some sort of surgical area. "Great," she breathed. "I hate blood more than I hate basements."

Using the edges of her fingernails, she eased open one side of the door and entered the sterile-smelling room. She had taken two steps when she heard a noise.

Closing her eyes, she listened above her ragged breathing and racing pulse. There it was again. Wasting no time, she followed the direction of the noise, letting it get louder and louder as she inched her way along the cold tile wall.

After what felt like an eternity, she found the door from behind which the noise was coming. *Damn!* she silently cursed when she saw there was a curtain over the small glass windowpane in the door. There were no options. The noise sounded too much like a painful groan to ignore.

Haley opened the door and very nearly screamed when she took in the sight.

Without hesitation, she rushed forward and yanked a strip of tape from Barbara's mouth.

"I hope you brought the troops," Barbara said.

"Just me," she answered in a whisper. "What have they done to her?" Haley asked as she went to the bedside and rubbed the hair away from Claire's bloated, lifeless-looking face. "Is she…"

"No," Barbara answered quickly. "She moans every now and again. Untie me and we'll carry her out of here."

"What about all these tubes?"

"They stay put."

Haley froze when she spun and looked into the cold eyes of the speaker.

Chapter Seventeen

"Detective Ross, what is the meaning of this?" Phelps said quietly as soon as he closed the wooden doors behind him. "I have dinner guests."

"Maybe they'll all throw in for your bail," Dalton thundered back.

"Keep your voice down," Phelps snarled, moving forward in the vestibule. "I don't know what you hope to accomplish by barging into my home but—"

"I talked to Lauer."

That statement seemed to take the starch out of Phelps's legs. He staggered backward into a chair.

"I see."

Dalton walked over and grabbed the lapels of the man's black dinner jacket. "I don't think you do."

"Do you require anything, sir?" the butler said, coming forward.

"That won't be necessary," Phelps answered. "Just see that my wife and our guests aren't disturbed. Make sure Olivia keeps the baby upstairs."

"Very well," he said with a polite nod before disappearing.

"You have about ten seconds to tell me where she is."

"I don't know," Phelps insisted. "I haven't heard from Claire since the day she—"

Dalton gave him a hard shake. "Don't screw with me, Phelps. I want to know what you did with Haley."

"Haley?" Phelps seemed genuinely surprised.

"If she has so much as an ingrown toenail," Dalton warned, "they won't be able to identify you with dental records."

"I promise you, Detective. I have no knowledge of anything Haley has done since she left the firm."

"Fine." Dalton shoved the man in the general direction of the front door. "Turn around."

"For what?"

"You're under arrest."

Phelps held up his hands. "I can explain everything."

Dalton reached back and took the cuffs from his belt loop. "You have exactly ten seconds."

"If they take the baby, it will kill my wife. I had no choice."

"Eight seconds," Dalton said. "What does your baby have to do with Haley?"

"Nothing," Phelps answered quickly. "I'm trying to explain why I helped Lawrence."

"Six seconds. Helped Lawrence do what?"

"Fabricate the police record on Claire Benedict. That's all I did."

"Three seconds. Not good enough. I want to know where Haley is and I want to know now."

"Arresting me won't help you, Detective. Talk to Lawrence Betterman. This was all his idea."

"One second left. What was?"

Dalton stopped counting the seconds as he listened to Phelps describe one of the most disgusting, brilliant scams he had heard in all his years on the force. "Did Betterman stab Haley?"

"I'm sure he didn't do it himself, but he knows enough of the wrong kind of people that it would have been a simple thing for him to make the arrangements."

"Finish your party and enjoy tonight," Dalton said, stepping past the quivering man. "If I find Haley and her friends in time, I'll only send you to prison."

"WHAT HAVE YOU DONE to Claire?" Haley demanded as she tried not to think about the gun pointed at her.

Dr. Dixon sucked in a breath. "She reacted to the medication."

"Medication for what?" Barbara asked.

"Tape her mouth until we know what he plans to do with them."

Barbara let out a whole list of suggestions before

the guard replaced the tape. Haley held Claire's hand, feeling the heat from a fever on her skin.

"She's burning up," Haley told him. "You're a doctor, how can you do this?"

"Shut up!"

"What do you want me to do with her?" the guard asked, pointing at Haley with the barrel of his gun.

"Bring her with us for the time being. She's his problem, not mine."

The guard tied her hands behind her back with a piece of rubber used in drawing blood, then she was taken to the first floor, into one of the locked rooms. It was filled with caged animals, computers and other machines. Every machine but a telephone, she thought ruefully as she tried to think of a possible escape. Whoever "he" was, she wasn't in any great hurry to meet him.

"Please tell me what is wrong with Claire?" Haley asked in a small voice.

"She's got a toxic case of overstimulation of the ovaries," Dixon said.

"Will she die?"

"Possibly," he said as calmly as if they were discussing an experiment on a lab rat instead of a human life. "But the harvest should still prove successful."

"Harvest?"

"With Miss Benedict's genes, we should be able to command top dollar for her donated eggs."

Haley's jaw dropped. "Claire isn't donating her

eggs. You're stealing them and killing her in the process.''

Dr. Dixon looked into her eyes. ''An unfortunate risk, and an uncommon one. We had never intended Ms. Benedict to find out, but it would seem your friend is a very thorough person.''

''Are you going to—''

''How did this happen!'' Betterman yelled, bursting into the room. ''It's going to look very suspicious to the police when all three of them disappear.''

''You?'' Haley gasped.

''Sorry to disappoint you, Ms. Jenkins. Please understand that it isn't personal. Business is business.''

''Your business is the law,'' she argued. ''How can you be involved with him?''

''Either shut up, Haley, or I'll have the good doctor give you something to keep you quiet.''

Haley stepped back, until she felt her hands make contact with the master panel for the bank of computers. Nervously, she flicked her fingernail along the smooth edges of the switches as Betterman went over and stood with Dixon.

''We have to change our strategy,'' Betterman told him. ''We no longer have the luxury of time. The detective assigned to the case is too close to Ms. Jenkins.''

Dixon looked up from the printout he had been studying. ''What are you saying?''

''We have to get rid of them.''

"Hold on, Lawrence. Our agreement included you finding me willing participants. I have never agreed to murder."

"Tell that to the Benedict woman," Betterman fired back. "You're the one who administered the drugs that are killing her."

"It was an adverse reaction," Dixon argued. "We'll still be able to harvest her eggs, and if she dies, I can still argue that she self-injected."

"Who will believe your argument when Ms. Jenkins and the Prather woman tell a different story?"

"Then we stop now," Dixon said. "She might be able to recover from the overdose and no one else will get hurt."

"You're being naive," Betterman yelled. "Besides, I already have buyers for the donor eggs. I've taken deposits."

"I warned you not to do that," Dixon said. "I'm not even sure she can last until the eggs reach maturity."

"You'd better hope she can," Betterman warned. He was about to continue his threats when his cell phone rang.

If Haley thought he looked murderous before, it was nothing like the blazing expression in his eyes when he turned on her.

"It would seem Ms. Jenkins has taken the situation out of our hands. Jonathan tells me that Detective Ross just left his house."

"What did he tell him?" Dixon asked.

"Everything."

"What do we do now?" Dixon wailed. "I'm not going to be a party to killing, Lawrence."

"Don't worry. I have an acquaintance who isn't quite so squeamish. I'll call him and get him over here now. If the detective shows up, stall."

As Betterman flipped open his cell phone, Haley flipped each switch on the board behind her. Luckily, nothing beeped or chimed, so Betterman had no idea what she had done. He only knew that he couldn't get his phone to work.

"I'm not getting reception," he growled. "Keep a close eye on her. I'll use the phone in your office. And you," he said to the guard, "go back to your post and make sure Detective Ross doesn't come storming in here until we've taken care of things."

"You can't let him kill us," Haley said to Dixon.

The doctor sat at one of the long tables, his head buried in his hands. "I never set out to hurt anyone. I've devoted my entire life to helping people give life."

"Then don't start taking it now," she pleaded. "Dalton knows whatever Phelps knows."

"I warned Lawrence about that."

"About what?"

"Phelps and his wife can't have children," he said.

"But they have a little girl."

"Thanks to a woman Lawrence picked up at the Rose Tattoo. I paid her five thousand dollars to act as surrogate."

"That is using your skills the right way," Haley assured him.

Dixon shook his head. "We told the girl the baby had died after birth. We tell them all that so our clients never run the risk of having their rights challenged later on. We let them keep the money, though."

Real big of you. "That was a kind gesture. Don't stop there, Doctor. You have to let me help Claire. She needs to be in an emergency room."

"I don't think she can be saved," Dixon admitted.

"We have to try," Haley pleaded. "Please? You don't want me dead, do you, Doctor?"

"Of course not, but..."

"But nothing. Dalton knows where I am. No matter what Betterman thinks up, Dalton will figure it out and you'll go to prison, maybe even worse."

"How did I get to this point?" Dixon whined.

Haley went to him. "I don't know how you got here, but I do know that you don't have to stay. Help me."

"He'll probably kill us all." Dixon sighed. "Lawrence needs the money. His ex-wife took everything."

"We don't have much time," Haley begged. "Untie me and help me get my friends out of here."

With resignation, Dixon untied her hands and showed her a back way to the staircase. "You're on your own, Ms. Jenkins," he said. "I can't help you."

"But Claire needs—"

"Last rites."

"THE SWAT TEAM has one male dressed like a guard near the door. There's also movement in one of the offices on the first floor and the sniper says he can make out a figure moving down the hallway. Over," announced the voice coming from the police radio.   Dalton smashed his fist against the hood of the car. "We need information on a woman. Just over five feet, long hair. Over."

"Sorry, Detective, the blinds make it impossible to tell. Over."

"Give me a jacket," Dalton called.

"You aren't going in there," his lieutenant said. "You know the rules, Ross. This is too personal for you to handle."

"Detective, we got a car coming toward the entrance. Over."

"Stop it," Dalton instructed. "I'll be right there. Keep it quiet out there. No sense in tipping our hand. Over."

Running through the woods that separated the parking lot from the road, Dalton arrived just in time to see one of the uniforms relieve the driver of a Tech-9.

"That's a lot of firepower," Dalton said as he turned the handcuffed man and braced him against the car. "Well, well. I think I just found my waterfront park stabber."

"You sure?"

"Absolutely," Dalton answered. "This is the guy who stabbed Haley in the park." He shoved back the man's hood before another officer handed him the guy's wallet. "So, Mr. Trent. We've got you on assault and illegal possession of a firearm. If any of those women are hurt, I'll make sure the D.A. changes the charge to attempted murder for the park and accessory to murder for tonight."

"Want me to run him?" the officer asked.

"By all means. If he's got a record, maybe the D.A. can nail him with the three-strikes rule so he'll never see the light of day again."

"Why are you pressing me?" the prisoner grumbled. "I'm just the grunt."

"Then start talking," Dalton suggested. "Maybe the D.A. will look kindly upon you." *Until I get finished talking,* he added mentally.

"The guy you want is Lawrence Betterman. He's a hotshot who doesn't like getting his hands dirty."

"Tell me something I don't know," Dalton countered.

"I'm supposed to meet him and pop three women."

"When?" Dalton asked.

"Now."

"Then, Mr. Trent, I suggest you get naked."

"What for?"

"If Betterman is expecting you, I won't keep him waiting."

"Hey, Dalton," the young officer began. "The lieutenant won't authorize this. You should—"

Dalton pulled Trent's black sweats on, making sure his flak jacket was well-hidden. "Give me a sixty-second lead, then radio over to the lieutenant. Consider that an order, just in case things go wrong and IA needs someone to blame."

"Dalton? Over?"

"Yeah? Over," he said into the radio handed to him.

"We've got a man on the roof. He reports shots fired. Over."

"WE'LL GO OUT the way I came in," Haley whispered.

"I never knew Claire was this heavy," Barbara said as they struggled to carry her up the stairs.

"She's bloated from whatever they gave her," Haley grunted. "We'll put her on a diet when she's better."

"Let's hope," Barbara whispered. "Her arm is still bleeding where we took out the IV."

"We can deal with that once we get out of here."

"Did you hear a shot?" Barbara asked, her green eyes filled with worry.

"Maybe we got lucky and Betterman blew his brains out."

"Or he killed Dixon and we're next."

"You aren't helping, Barbara. Think positive."

"Right," Barbara agreed. "How much farther?"

"A few more steps and then we have to get to the office."

"I feel like my arms are being ripped from my body."

"That isn't a positive thought," Haley said as she balanced Claire's upper body against her knee while she turned the knob. "Be quiet now."

Haley felt perspiration trickle between her shoulder blades as they reached the office. She opened the door and had taken a couple of steps inside when a shot shattered the glass near Barbara's head.

"Hurry!" Haley yelled. "Get out the window and I'll pass her down to you."

"But—"

"Don't argue, Barbara! Move!"

Haley hoisted Claire over her shoulder with a great deal of effort. The sound of footfalls became louder and closer. "Hurry, Barbara!"

Haley went to the window and as soon as Barbara hit the soft earth, she leaned forward and dropped Claire like a sack. She lifted her leg to make her escape when she felt a hand grab her hair and tug.

The stench of gunpowder reached her nostrils as Betterman wrenched her away from the window.

Seeing him point the gun in the direction of the ground beneath the window, Haley simply reacted. Gathering what little strength she had left, she stomped on his instep.

"Run, Barbara!"

"Damn, you!" Betterman seethed.

"Ouch!" Haley yelled when he pulled her hair hard enough to bring tears to her eyes. Haley blinked, then saw the shadowy figure in the doorway. "No," she whispered softly.

"Put the gun down, Betterman. There are about fifty cops crawling all over this place. Dixon is already dead. He ate his gun."

Dalton was dressed all in black and there was a cut above his left eye.

"You are persistent," Betterman said as he yanked Haley so that she was directly in Dalton's line of fire. "I knew I should have shot you again just for good measure."

"You're right," he answered with deadly calm. "Let her go."

Betterman gave a bitter little laugh. "She's going to make sure I get out of this in one piece. Call off your friends and I'll need transportation to the Caymans."

"The only transportation you'll need is a hearse."

"Shoot me," Haley said to Dalton.

A flicker of emotion flashed in his eyes as he continued to block the door with his wide stance, gun thrust forward.

"Didn't you see that movie *Speed?*" she asked. "I'm his leverage. Get rid of me and he has no power."

"He can't shoot you, Haley. My associate took an entire roll of film of the two of you. He can't. But just in case, I'll make sure he doesn't turn into a problem."

Haley watched in silent horror as Betterman's finger began to squeeze the trigger.

"No!"

The explosion blinded her. The sound was deafening. Then she felt a searing pain in her leg just before Betterman's bullet hit Dalton squarely in the chest.

"I CAN'T BELIEVE you shot me," Haley said, giving Dalton's hand a squeeze.

"I was only doing what you said. Besides, I made sure I wouldn't hit anything vital."

"My thigh is vital to me."

"Flesh wound," he dismissed, glad to find her in such good spirits. "The hungry little insects did more damage than my little bullet."

"I'll try to remember that the next time I put on a bathing suit and I have that lovely scar showing."

He winked at her. "Just so long as you show it to me."

Dalton dropped her hand and moved closer to her hospital bed. He would have climbed in with her if he hadn't been afraid of disturbing all the tubes and monitors. "Am I allowed to say the words yet?"

Her lips fell open. Her eyes reminded him of those of a startled fawn caught in headlights. "Not yet."

He was disappointed, but she hadn't said, "Don't ever." He reached down and gently drew her against his taut body. His mouth found hers and he savored the feel and taste of her.

Seeing her in the clutches of that madman was a memory he wanted desperately to forget. The feel of her body against his was doing a great job of making him forget everything except his love for this incredibly strong woman.

Reluctantly, he lifted his head. His fingers brushed a few strands of hair from her flushed face. "I'm only allowed a few minutes."

"I know," she breathed as her small palm rested against his jaw. "I thought Betterman had killed you. I saw—"

"You saw how well a vest protects a cop."

"What if he had aimed for your head?"

"I'd have jumped up, or ducked."

"I'm not kidding, Dalton. What you do is..."

"No more dangerous than a civilian taking the law into her own hands," he said as he took her palm and graced it with a kiss. "You should have called me."

"You would have needed a warrant. I didn't."

"We could have worked together."

"No," she reminded him, giggling when he tickled her with his tongue. "I only would have gotten you in trouble. Maybe even cost you your job."

"I'll be riding a desk for a while now," he admitted. "My boss thought I acted irresponsibly and he'd like to fry me for shooting you."

"I'll talk to him," she said as she kissed his mouth. "He'll just have to accept the fact that I was insistent."

"I'm feeling a little insistent myself," he told her as he kissed a portion of her exposed neck. "How long are they going to keep you here?"

"I can't believe you're trying to seduce an invalid. I'll ring for the nur—"

When she stopped abruptly and lay down looking guilty, Dalton glanced over his shoulder and found one of the nurses standing in the doorway. "I was just leaving," Dalton lied.

"It isn't that," she said as a minister appeared at her side. "The Reverend Norris needs to see you, Miss Jenkins."

"I'll stay," Dalton said as he reached for her hand.

Haley flinched and pulled her hand away from him. "No. I want you to go."

"But Haley?"

"Leave, Dalton. I'll call you."

He took one long look at her, knowing somehow

that it would be his last. Unshed tears filled her eyes but the remainder of her face was a void. He paused at the door, hoping she might change her mind. She didn't.

Dalton left the room. The last thing he heard was her gut-wrenching scream when the hospital chaplain informed her that Claire Benedict had died.

Epilogue

"The funeral was more than a month ago," Shelby said gently. "We're all starting to get worried."

"Thanks." Haley twirled the ice in her glass with a straw. "I'm sure I'll snap out of it soon."

"Dylan told me that Betterman and Phelps have both decided to plead guilty."

"Yep. They didn't have much choice."

"You must be relieved."

Haley met her friend's inquisitive eyes. "Relieved?"

"Sure, if you don't have to testify, then you can continue avoiding Dalton."

"I'm not avoiding him," Haley said, hedging. "I'm trying to get over him. I won't be able to do that if I have to see him."

"Are you in love with him?"

"Yes."

"Then why are you torturing yourself?"

"I saw him shot, Shelby. You, better than anyone,

should understand how I feel. I don't want to live my life wondering every time he leaves the house whether he'll come home again.''

"Believe it or not, you get used to it.''

"I'm not like you, Shelby. I don't think I could stand it if anything happened to Dalton.''

"I'm not in any hurry to see my husband come to any harm.''

Haley cringed. "I didn't mean it like that. I just meant that you are a really independent person. You went after Chad's kidnapper like a bear.''

"And you put two very terrible men in prison and saved Barbara's life. You're a lot stronger than you might think. Especially if you have someone like Dalton at your side.''

"Claire died.''

"Claire would have died anyway, Haley. I know what the medical examiner's report said. There wasn't anything you could have done differently.''

"Maybe if I'd have pushed harder at the beginning, gotten to her sooner.''

"Pushed for what? Betterman had Claire call you to put your mind at ease. Then he paid to have you stabbed. You'll drive yourself crazy if you keep this up.''

"I know.'' Haley sighed. "I'm making myself physically ill. I'm either throwing up or I can't seem to haul myself out of bed. I still haven't even put forth the effort to start a new practice.''

"Back up," Rose said as she joined them. "Tired and throwing up?"

Haley smiled weakly. "I'm thinking of writing a book—*The Crisis Diet: How to Lose Weight after a Major Catastrophe.*"

"Have you lost weight?" Rose asked.

"Not really, I... Oh my heavens."

"It's going to be tough to avoid Dalton Ross now," Shelby said with a smile.

HALEY WAS IN THE MIDDLE of comparing swatches of wallpaper when the doorbell rang. Shoving her hair out of her eyes, she left the samples in the empty room she planned to use as a nursery and started down the stairs. She prayed it wasn't another group of misdirected tourists. Ever since Thanksgiving, it seemed as if a never-ending stream of people had mistaken her home for the one next door, which *was* part of the walking tour.

She opened the door with a manufactured smile. It vanished instantly when she saw Dalton standing on her doorstep.

Tugging on her oversize sweatshirt, she positioned herself off to the side, hoping to hide her burgeoning midsection. "What brings you by?"

"Unrequited love."

Haley closed her eyes and silently prayed for strength. It wasn't easy, not when she opened her eyes to find him staring at her. It was almost as intimate as being touched.

"Are you going to invite me in?"

"This isn't a good time."

"It will be soon," he said pointedly as he waltzed into the house.

"Do come in," she muttered. "Really, Dalton. I'm in the middle of a project."

"Really?" he asked with a sigh as he kept right on going until he plopped himself down at the kitchen table. "What sort of project are you working on?"

"I…um…decorating."

Dalton smiled as his keen amber eyes continued to follow her every move. She decided it was safer if she sat across from him, at least then he might not notice the change in her appearance.

"Decorating what?"

"A room."

"Which room?"

"Why are you here?" she asked as she felt a pang of uncertainty tingle in her stomach.

"I had a drink with Dylan Tanner last night."

"Why?" *Oh God, he knew!*

Dalton shrugged. "He wanted to have a heart-to-heart with me."

"About what?" she asked, measuring her words carefully.

"It seems he went through a similar situation with Shelby."

He knows!

"It wasn't the same at all," Haley assured him.

Dalton's cheerful smile dulled. "I have a theory about us. Care to hear it?"

"Do I have to?"

"Yes."

If he says he'll pay support and wants to take the baby away from me every other weekend, I'll die.

"I'll take your silence as approval. See, I think you've lost a lot of people in your thirty-six years."

"Thirty-five," she corrected.

"Whatever." He sighed patiently. "You won't give me a chance because you think I'll die too."

"You *are* a cop."

"A very bright, resourceful and careful one."

"That's why Betterman was able to shoot you."

"Special circumstances," he scoffed. "I took a bit of a chance because it was you."

"Don't do this. Please?"

"I told Dylan you would say that."

"Then respect how I feel and leave...me alone."

With lightning speed, Dalton stood, rounded the table and knelt beside her. "Believe me, I would if I could," he said as he took her hands. "I can't, Haley. I can't think of anything but you. I love you so much that it hurts."

She tried to pull her hands away. "I'm sure you'll get over it."

"I tried, but it didn't work."

"Try harder."

"I even thought about giving up my job," he said as he lifted her knuckles to his mouth. When she shivered, his eyes glowed triumphantly. "I will if that is what it takes to have you in my life."

"I would never ask that of you," she whispered, unwillingly enjoying the strength of his touch.

"Then what, Haley? Tell me what it would take."

Her chest grew tight and she felt her eyes begin to burn. "There is no answer for us. It just won't work."

Releasing her hands, Dalton dropped his head into her lap. She felt him chuckle before he said, "So you tried to forget me with food, huh?"

He seemed to freeze for a minute, then stood and reached out to place his palm against her belly. "Haley?" He said her name in a choked whisper.

She held her breath, looked at his mouth, his penetrating eyes.

His palms smoothed over her body, molding and cherishing. He met her eyes and asked, "I guess being pregnant has made it impossible for you to forget me."

He looked stricken and her heart broke. "Don't look so horrified, Dalton. I don't have any plans to— What are you doing?"

"Taking Dylan's advice."

"Dylan told you to carry me up the stairs?"

"He told me to try communicating with you."

"And that requires heavy lifting?"

"I didn't know you were going to be this heavy."

"Gee, thanks."

"I meant that in the nicest possible way, of course."

"Of course," she grumbled when he pushed open her bedroom door and gently placed her on the bed. "We can't do this," she said when he joined her.

Dalton reached his hand under her shirt and then his eyes grew serious. "*Can't* as in you refuse to admit that you love me? Or *can't* because it isn't safe for the baby?"

Haley said nothing.

"God, you smell sweet," he said as he tasted the skin at her throat. "You feel good, too."

"Dalton." She murmured his name and his hand stilled.

"Don't stop me, Haley. Not now."

"I wasn't going to stop you. I was going to agree with you."

Lifting himself up on one arm, he asked, "So you think communicating on this level is the best place for us to start?"

"No. I have refused to admit that I love you."

"Do you?"

Haley touched his cheek. "Very much."

"Know something?" Dalton said with a grin.

"What?"

"You talk too much."

*Turn the page for a bonus look at
what's in store for you in the next
ROSE TATTOO.*

It's a sneak preview of

A MOTHER'S ARMS

by Kelsey Roberts

February, 1998

Prologue

"Do you really think she'll show?"

Leaning back against his high-backed leather chair, he quietly regarded his visitor as he pondered the question. "I think Miss Hannah Bailey poses a real threat, don't you?"

His visitor began to squirm in the seat as small beads of perspiration formed on his brow and upper lip. "I don't think she can find anything. Not after all this time."

"Have you been able to determine which child she is?"

He shook his head. "Not yet, but I have it narrowed down to three or four probables."

"Probables?" he repeated softly. "I paid you well to make certain nothing like this ever happened."

"I know," the man babbled.

He hated babbling. It was so weak.

"When will you know if she has, in fact, made good on her threats to come to Charleston?"

"I sent a man to New Orleans to keep an eye on her. He left this morning."

"I have a copy of her letter," he said as he patiently unfolded the crisp, white document and passed it across his desk. "It would appear that Miss Bailey has contacted every social services agency and every courthouse in the state looking for answers."

"It won't matter. Even if she does manage to get something, the records were doctored even before they were filed. She can't trace anything back to us."

"Us?" He rose, sighing deeply as he did. "There is no *us*. There hasn't been for nearly twenty years. I'm in no position to have the past come back to haunt me now, do you understand?"

The man's face flushed with anger, but he knew better than to go on the offensive. "What do you want me to do?"

"I want you to stay away from me. I can't have you dropping in on me."

"What am I supposed to do if she comes snooping around here?"

"If Miss Bailey is so determined to trace her biology, it would seem only fitting that she meet the same fate as her mother."

The man's flush drained until his face was nearly as white as his shirt. "You want me to kill her?"

A woman alone—
What can she do...?
Whom can she trust...?
Where can she run...?
Straight into the arms of

HER PROTECTOR

By popular demand we bring you the exciting reprise of
the women-in-jeopardy theme you loved. Don't miss

#430 *THE SECOND MRS. MALONE*
by Amanda Stevens (August)

#433 *STORM WARNINGS*
by Judi Lind (September)

#438 *LITTLE GIRL LOST*
by Adrianne Lee (October)

When danger lurks around every corner, there's only
one place you're safe...in the strong, sheltering arms
of the man who loves you.

**Look for all the books in the
HER PROTECTOR miniseries!**

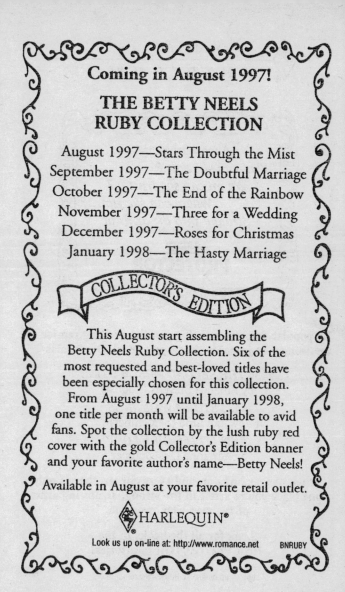

Coming in August 1997!

THE BETTY NEELS RUBY COLLECTION

August 1997—Stars Through the Mist
September 1997—The Doubtful Marriage
October 1997—The End of the Rainbow
November 1997—Three for a Wedding
December 1997—Roses for Christmas
January 1998—The Hasty Marriage

COLLECTOR'S EDITION

This August start assembling the
Betty Neels Ruby Collection. Six of the
most requested and best-loved titles have
been especially chosen for this collection.
From August 1997 until January 1998,
one title per month will be available to avid
fans. Spot the collection by the lush ruby red
cover with the gold Collector's Edition banner
and your favorite author's name—Betty Neels!

Available in August at your favorite retail outlet.

HARLEQUIN®

You meet a man. He's so appealing,
so sexy. He's your soul mate, the man
you've waited your whole life to find.
But you get the sense he's hiding
something...and it's not just
his feelings....

HIDDEN IDENTITY

You meet some of the sexiest and most secretive men
in the HIDDEN IDENTITY series. These men may talk
a good game, but their kisses never lie! Find out who
the real men are in HIDDEN IDENTITY!

Don't miss the next exciting title:

#434 BEN'S WIFE
by Charlotte Douglas
September 1997

Don't miss any of the exciting HIDDEN IDENTITY
stories—only from Harlequin Intrigue!

Let's Celebrate!

LOVE & LAUGHTER™

invites you to the party of the season!

Grab your popcorn and be prepared to laugh as we celebrate with **LOVE & LAUGHTER**.

Harlequin's newest series is going Hollywood!

Let us make you laugh with three months of terrific books, authors and romance, plus a chance to win a FREE 15-copy video collection of the best romantic comedies ever made.

For more details look in the back pages of any Love & Laughter title, from July to September, at your favorite retail outlet.

Don't forget the popcorn!

Available wherever
Harlequin books are sold.

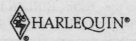 HARLEQUIN®

Look us up on-line at: http://www.romance.net

LLCELEB

HARLEQUIN WOMEN KNOW ROMANCE WHEN THEY SEE IT.

And they'll see it on **ROMANCE CLASSICS**, the new 24-hour TV channel devoted to romantic movies and original programs like the special **Harlequin®** **Showcase of Authors & Stories**.

The **Harlequin®** **Showcase of Authors & Stories** introduces you to many of your favorite romance authors in a program developed exclusively for Harlequin® readers.

Watch for the **Harlequin®** **Showcase of Authors & Stories** series beginning in the summer of 1997.

If you're not receiving ROMANCE CLASSICS, call your local cable operator or satellite provider and ask for it today!

Escape to the network of your dreams.

HARLEQUIN AND SILHOUETTE
ARE PLEASED TO PRESENT

Love, marriage—and the pursuit of family!

Check your retail shelves for these upcoming titles:

July 1997
Last Chance Cafe by Curtiss Ann Matlock
The most determined bachelor in Oklahoma is in trouble! A lovely widow with three daughters has moved next door—and the girls want a dad! But he wants to know if their mom needs a husband....

August 1997
Thorne's Wife by Joan Hohl
Pennsylvania. It was only to be a marriage of convenience—until they fell in love! Now, three years later, tragedy threatens to separate them forever and Valerie wants only to be in the strength of her husband's arms. For she has some very special news for the expectant father...

September 1997
Desperate Measures by Paula Detmer Riggs
New Mexico judge Amanda Wainwright's daughter has been kidnapped, and the price of her freedom is a verdict in favor of a notorious crime boss. So enters ex-FBI agent Devlin Buchanan—ruthless, unstoppable—and soon there is no risk he will not take for her.

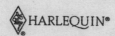